GROWING UP WITH EVIL

M.E. Fenos

ISBN 978-1-63784-660-5 (paperback)
ISBN 978-1-63784-661-2 (digital)

Hawes & Jenkins Publishing
16427 N Scottsdale Road Suite 410
Scottsdale, AZ 85254
www.hawesjenkins.com

Printed in the United States of America

Dedicated to Michael A. Fenos. I shall forever appreciate your love, kindness, strength, protection, and unwavering support.

Artemus. His friends called him Artie. Artie was a good-looking man, dark features, deep brown eyes, effortlessly in shape, not muscular, just fit. Artie came to America from Italy when he was ten years old. His dad had the bluest eyes, a thick head of white hair and a sly smile. He worked in concrete, was sergeant of arms at the local Italian club (basically he made sure no one got into the club that shouldn't), made salami, homemade wine and spoke very little English.

Artie's mom was a slender woman with beautiful red hair and brown eyes, she too spoke very little English but that didn't hinder her enjoyment of America. Their neighborhood was flush with Italian Americans making them feel right at home. The neighborhood church was an old Italian church which added to the ease of the transition.

Artie's mom was what one might call an "authentic" cook, making the most scrumptious Italian foods effortlessly. She had an impressive garden growing herbs and vegetables in abundance, weather permitting she would take Artie and his sisters outside while she worked in her garden while occasionally tossing ripe tomatoes to Artie to enjoy, knowing he was 'secretly' sneaking all he wanted.

It wasn't until the age of 44 that Helen's mom became pregnant for the second time. They never tried *not* to get pregnant, yet it took nearly 24 years for a second pregnancy. With 24 years between children, it was as if Helen was an only child reaping the benefits of her parents' full attention. Helen's blue eyes and light brown hair were very complimentary to her small features.

Making friends and school came easy to Helen, she was a simply pretty girl, not obvious, but gently pretty. After graduation Helen worked for a greeting card company as a secretary, a job that wasn't too exciting, but it was a paycheck and afforded her the freedom to buy things for herself and extra cash to spend time with her friends on the weekends.

Artie dropped out of school in the 8th grade and went to work for his dad in the cement business learning to pour driveways, patios, build fireplaces and even homes was exciting for Artie.

Artie's dad knew his son was going to be a good provider, he was quickly becoming a skilled craftsman, but pushed for him to get more schooling. Instead of school, Artie chose to join the Marines which allowed him to continue his education outside of the school setting where he learned valuable lessons on life, consequences, and skill.

He was gifted with natural intelligence and an overwhelming curiosity. His fellow soldiers liked being around Artie who was quick to make them laugh, that, and being the cook increased his popularity with the troops. He made friendships that would last a lifetime.

Artie had been out of the Marine Corps for about a year before he met Helen at a local restaurant where he was meeting up with friends. Helen was there with a group of her friends one of which was dating a friend of Artie's. Artie introduced himself to Helen and that was all it took. Their first date solidified they were done dating others, seeing one another nearly every day after that first meeting.

The romance was a whirlwind, the marriage just months after their first meeting. Easily falling in love with the handsome Marine who was always quick with a joke, kind, and eager to help those in need.

The wedding at St. Michael's church was breathtaking. The stain-glassed windows filtering in hints of color showcasing the light dust in the air bouncing off the intricately detailed pews. Artie's twin sisters Giana and Maria served as flower girls and were so delicately lovely as they bounced down the aisle in matching yellow tea-length ball gowns adorned silk rose appliques around the neckline.

Helen made her way down the aisle in a ballerina style gown that settled at her ankles the neckline was round with faux pearls, adorning her perfectly coiffed hair a tiara fit for a princess with a short veil falling to her shoulders. Artie was pleasantly stunned by his beautiful almost wife, the smile on his face nearly reached his ears. Artie wore a classic black tuxedo that fit like a glove enhancing his muscular arms, Helen stared a bit longer than necessary at her handsome man. The vows and rings were exchanged followed by a tender kiss to the enjoyment of the guests.

The reception was held in the basement of the church the food prepared by family with music provided by Artie's friends who played at local festivals. The wedding wasn't "showy" it was all about family and love. Artie and Helen left the wedding reception earlier than the rest of the guests in a car with a huge "just married" sign smothered with balloons. The guests enjoyed the food and drink then made their way home as Artie and Helen's parents stayed to clean, stack chairs, and pack up leftovers.

Artie had a good job working for the city and insisted his wife did not need to work. Helen loved that idea and spent her days crocheting lovely blankets, cleaning the home, and getting dinner prepared. Helen's parents would often visit, her mom would help prepare dinner teaching Helen to make some of their family's favorite dishes.

Helen's parents were of Polish descent, so many of the dinners were new to Artie. Artie enjoyed cooking and food, so he was enthusiastic to try new foods and liked most of them. Artie's mom came over to show Helen how to make some of Artie's favorite Italian dishes. One simple dish that was inexpensive to make was gnocchi and Helen enjoyed learning new sauces and the use of herbs directly from her mother-in-law's garden. Cooking with the windows open was almost cruel to the neighbors who could smell the delicious aromas wafting through the gentle breeze.

Artie and Helen were married at a time when the man worked outside the home and the woman was the homemaker and caretaker of the children. They were both anxious to start a family and hoped to have many children. It wasn't long before their family began to grow.

Welcoming a son after their first year of marriage was a Blessing. Matteo was their pride and joy. A handsome baby with a gentle disposition, olive skin and a full head of black hair. Artie was so proud to show off his son to everyone, including strangers. His favorite comments were the ones that would point out that Matteo looked just like his daddy. Artie's parents visited regularly, probably more than Helen would have liked. They adored their grandson and wanted to be with him as much as possible, it was their first grandchild, and they wanted to give him the world.

A few years later Jean was born on a cool spring day. Giving birth to Jean was a longer delivery than expected but with the epidural it was pain-free, so Helen had no complaints. Jean was a fussy baby, plain looking with a larger than normal nose. Helen would tease she had an "Italian" nose. Jean didn't look Italian with her pale complexion and light sparse strands of hair not the full head of hair like her brother. She resembled Helen's family more than Artie's Italian family.

Matteo was gentle with his new little sister and enjoyed holding her when Helen was preparing bottles or getting meals prepared. The new parents discussed having the children close in age, knowing it would be hard at first, but believing the kids would benefit from having a brother or sister close in age to play with, share experiences, and attend the same schools creating a strong bond. Something Helen missed being 24 years younger than her brother.

The plan to have the children close in age was agreeable for both, although the arrival of Tonya was a surprise coming exactly 1 year and 3 days after Jean. She was bigger than most babies, so big the newborn clothes Helen was hoping to pass on from Jean, didn't fit. Luckily Artie added a part time job to his already busy schedule, so Helen was able to splurge on a few new outfits for Tonya. A few weeks after Tonya was brought home, it was learned she had colic. The plan to have them close together didn't seem like such a great idea now. It was a lot to handle taking care of a toddler, a baby and a newborn that suffered from colic.

The constant wailing was very draining on Helen. Jean needed a lot of care being just a baby herself when Tonya cried, Jean cried making for a very stressful home. Matteo would soothe Jean by talking to her and petting her head which worked most of the time and when that didn't work, Helen would have Matteo feed her a bottle. Helen relied on Matteo more than she should, he was a toddler taking on grown-up responsibilities.

When Artie came home, he would do his best to help comfort Tonya, when he held her, she seemed angry, and her face became so red and distorted it worried Artie. Knowing that Helen may not be able to handle the children and their needs when Tonya required so much comforting Artie enlisted the help of the one person, he knew could handle anything…his mom. Artie's mom started to come over to the house several days a week to help with the babies. His sisters made a point of coming over after work to do the laundry and help with household chores. Helen was grateful for the help and the opportunity to sneak in a nap.

As the months passed Tonya's colic subsided making it easier for Helen, she was beyond relieved to be able to get some rest – not quite peace and quiet with three small children, but it was manageable, and she loved being a mother. Her daily routine fell quickly into place and her children were all well cared for thanks to Artie's mother and sisters.

Although three babies were a lot of work Artie and Helen were pleased with their growing family. Artie was hoping for another son, he and Helen always wanted a large family. Helen was overjoyed to announce to Artie they were expecting. This would be three babies in 3 years! Eh what's one more, Artie would joke.

Elena was born on a sweltering summer day. Artie had hoped for another son, when looking at this beautiful baby, Artie had zero complaints. Their family was now complete. Artie's mom was quick to come to stay for the first 3 weeks after Elena was born, caring the other children, and ensuring Helen was able to relax.

Elena was a pretty baby. She resembled Artie's Italian family. Elena's olive skin, dark eyes and soft features made her a beautiful baby. Artie and Helen were thrilled, and a bit concerned because she was just so quiet. Different from their other daughters. Matteo loved Elena instantly. He was good with his little sisters always their protector. Jean and Tonya were disinterested with Elena's arrival and paid her no attention. They didn't care to share anything with another baby, the two had displayed a selfish side even before they could speak. Helen brushed off their indifference because they too were just babies, believing they would eventually bond with Elena as they grew older.

Although they both hoped for a large family, as most people would consider four kids a large family, they realized four kids was more than enough. Helen would not be having any more children. Helen felt as though she was spreading herself too thin when it came to spending time with the children equally, she didn't like to have to rely on Artie's mom and sisters to come over to help her care for her children, cook and do housework. For now, she needed the help, but knew as the children grew her life would be more relaxed.

Matteo was five when Elena was born so he was some help to Helen. Matteo would help clean, feed his sisters and was quick to comfort a squawking Jean, or stop Tonya from playing with the oven.

Although things were still on the hectic side Helen limited visits from Artie's family saying she can take care of the house herself and the kids were much easier to care for now that Matteo can help. It was routine to have Jean and Tonya together for feedings, diaper changes, etc., Matteo was self-sufficient, it was almost sad how he never complained and was happy to lend a hand with whatever was needed. Elena was effortless and quiet, so it was easy to forget she too needed care, almost an afterthought to Helen. The downside of being a good baby is the possibility of being overlooked by a busy mom.

A few years passed and things were getting much easier. At 4 years old Jean was finally potty trained, Tonya still had several 'accidents', at 2 Elena was a prodigy quickly out of diapers and into big girl pants. Artie believed Tonya was probably wetting the bed for attention he just couldn't grasp why it would take her so long when Matteo and Elena were quick to learn.

Helen told him it's not fair to compare and that all children learn at their own pace, Helen secretly questioned this as well, she spent the most time with the two girls because they seemed to need more help and with Matteo and Elena being as good as they were, it was easy to give the two girls more attention. Helen had a tinge of guilt knowing she has four kids and, it wasn't fair not to be attentive to all her children.

Wondering if limiting the visits from Artie's family was the right thing to do, they were a huge help whenever they came over, yet Helen felt "less-than" because she couldn't do it alone. She dared not mention that she felt she needed help raising her kids or cleaning the house that would be an incredible insult to her mothering/housewife skills.

Artie never mentioned when the house was in disarray or dinner wasn't done when he came home from work, he would just clean whatever needed cleaning, finish making dinner, have Matteo help set the table and everything would fall into place.

Artie knew that Matteo and Elena took after him, they were obviously brighter than the other two. Make no mistake, he loved all his children and wouldn't have minded having another four kids. It was just a bit of an adjustment for him to have to expect less from the two girls than he did from Elena and Matteo.

There was times Artie would attempt to coax the two girls into sitting with him to learn to read or play. They avoided him as if being with him were a punishment. Being slow learners wasn't the only obstacle for the two girls, their defiant behavior was also an issue. Never cared to please anyone "No!" was their favorite response. Again, Helen would brush their behavior off as "terrible 2s…terrible 3s…"

Artie believed they were just terrible, unruly, something wasn't clicking with the two of them, they lacked kindness, a gentleness, even a simple appreciation for others which saddened him to know his children were so different. Why would they not be easy and carefree like Matteo and Elena? It was hard not to compare the children when they have the same parents, same upbringing, and same opportunities.

Other than the difficulty in connecting with Jean and Tonya, things were good. The family was growing, this time it was Artie's sister. Maria had been married for four years and just gave birth to a son, naming him Percy after her husband's father. The baby was an adorable miniature version of his daddy and the sweetest chubby face that defied you *not* to fall in love. Maria was an amazing mother very protective and doting on her darling baby.

Artie was a proud uncle and pleased that his kids would have a cousin. Giana's family grew as well, her husband was a handsome Frenchman his accent forced one to listen to every single word he spoke as each syllable seemed to carry a wealth of grandeur. It would be twins for Giana, two girls, Sophia and Bianca. Helen found time to crochet her new nephew and nieces cozy baby blankets and had them ready in time for their first visit. Percy was two months old, and the girls were just a few weeks old when Artie brought his children to his mom's house to meet their cousins.

Elena was propped on the corner of the sofa with pillows surrounding her as they placed Percy in her arms. Her gentle touches were deliberate as she looked at him in awe. The sweetness of the moment was not lost on Artie who teared up as he witnessed the pure love Elena showed Percy. Artie held Sophia and Bianca and sat next to Elena as she touched their tiny fingers and with the breath of an angel kissed their soft cheeks.

Matteo was allowed to hold the babies without the support of the pillows because he was a "big boy" overjoyed to have cousins he loved them instantly. Jean and Tonya wouldn't go by the babies hiding behind Helen as if the babies were going to hurt them. Artie thought it best not to encourage the girls, if they didn't want to see the babies or cuddle them it was probably for the best. The cousins all shared a similar look - olive skin, dark features, dark hair they looked like Matteo and Elena.

Jean and Tonya didn't look like their siblings or their cousins, they did look like one another, pale freckled faces, large features, sparse hair not quite resembling Helen's family either, more a mix of the less-flattering features found somewhere in the family tree. It wasn't just their looks that made them similar, it was their behavior, attitude, indifference, something about them seemed bad/off.

More times than she would care to admit to herself, Helen sat on the bathroom floor crying at her failure as a mother to Tonya and Jean, questioning where she went wrong. They laughed, but only when someone was upset, fell, or injured in some way. They didn't play like other kids appearing to be loners who only tolerated one another's company. The two appeared void of joy.

They would oftentimes knock something over, tear something up, spill whatever was in reach then blame Elena. Between household chores, meals and caring for the children it was easier for Helen to punish Elena when the two blamed her rather than trying to observe what was really happening. Remove the problem child from the others and that would eliminate the problem.

At two years old Elena didn't understand why she was being disciplined. Jean and Tonya found their favorite pastime. Wreak havoc - blame Elena. It seemed even from toddler stage there was a divide between the children. The two girls were always together, not that they were happy together it was as if they had an understanding. They condoned and fed off the other's lack of emotions and bullying.

It's unfathomable that 3- and 4-year-olds can be so mean, calculated, heck, it's a stretch to say but…smart even. Helen was beginning to believe that Elena was a bit of a handful and would keep her confined to her crib for most of the day so she wouldn't have to deal with any messes or incessant screaming from Jean and Tonya about whatever misdeed Elena was involved with. At times Helen was visibly overwhelmed with the chores and the children. Keeping Elena confined lessened her burden.

Now that Elena was hidden away in the bedroom the children were well-behaved for the most part as it was hard to blame Elena for anything when she's stuck in a crib. Helen kept up with her daily chores, Jean and Tonya would entertain themselves with cartoons, toys, sneaking snacks, anything that would give Helen time to get laundry done or meals cooked – Jean and Tonya had an internal clock and knew when lunch should be ready. Helen was sure to have their food ready to avoid the tantrums.

Tonya and Jean often spent time sneaking where they shouldn't. Tonya's favorite pastime was playing with the stove. Helen had to remove the knobs from the stove to prevent Tonya from turning the on the burners. When Artie questioned why the knobs were missing, she explained it was precautionary to stop Tonya from playing with the stove. Artie didn't find it excusable and felt as though Helen should have been able to keep a better watch over the children or teach Tonya that it was wrong to play with the stove.

He asked his mother to stop by the home every now and again because no child, especially Elena, should be made to spend their days in a crib. He hoped his mother would be able to reign in the other two girls and keep an eye on their questionable behavior.

Helen allowed Elena to be out of the crib if the grandmother was at the home, she wasn't sure if Artie had told his mom that Elena spent most of her day in the crib and felt she would judge her for confining Elena.

The grandmother was a huge help to Helen and was quick to make dinner and help clean the house. Helen called her sisters-in-law to cover for keeping Elena in the crib – just in case Artie had mentioned something to them.

Helen shared stories of how difficult Elena could be, she was always breaking something or getting into something she shouldn't. They didn't know why Helen believed Elena was difficult, she was a quiet, kind, happy little girl, quite effortless, very affectionate, and always smiling. A joy to be around.

Artie's sisters did notice how the other two daughters treated Elena. They never mentioned to Helen when they witnessed Tonya or Jean showing anger, being disruptive or defiant, they didn't want Helen to feel badly or feel as though they were criticizing her parenting. Once they reprimanded the girls telling them to be nice and when they did, in unison the two cried as if they were struck. Helen came to their rescue believing the aunts had punished them with a spank or a slap, which wasn't the case.

To see the little girls in action was disturbing, how they mastered the art of manipulation was unnerving. The difference between the children was evident Matteo and Elena were quiet, helpful, sweet, loving. Jean and Tonya were not. Every moment spent with Elena, they never saw her do anything deserving of punishment knowing the other two were always into something and should be sitting in time-out or put in their rooms. The aunts learned quickly not to attempt to discipline their nieces to avoid causing a divide with Helen. They also never left their children alone in a room with the two girls at any family gathering.

As for Jean and Tonya their obvious disdain for Elena was something Matteo noticed, and he quickly became her protector. He was always helping his sisters with whatever they needed. Matteo did his best not to leave Elena alone with Jean and Tonya, he felt she wasn't "safe" with them, he didn't know why they didn't like Elena. They were quick to stick their tongue out at Elena, give her a push or knock her over, anything to disrupt Elena's peace.

As Matteo, Jean and Tonya were ready for elementary school there was less need for their grandmother to help. Artie's mom prepared dinners several times a week, she enjoyed coming over to see Elena and spend time with her in the kitchen while Helen rested. Elena would balance on a chair and help her grandma roll out gnocchi, smash tomatoes and create dinner. It was as if Elena was witnessing magic, her eyes so big and smile so grand, it was beauty to see the sheer joy. Grandma bragged to Artie that Elena was a natural with a gift of cooking.

Grandma would take Elena to her home every now and again to show off her plentiful garden. The garden packed with herbs, the smell of basil as you walked the pathway to the tomatoes made Elena stop. Grandma knew she was enjoying the scents and in her very broken English would do her best to explain the herbs to Elena. When grandpa was home it was always a lunch of homemade salami, cheese, and wine. "Fake" wine for Elena as she enjoyed watered down Kool-Aid. The moments spent with her grandparents were simple, and at the same time significantly impactful. Her grandparents loved having her over telling Artie she could live with them forever he told them her sisters would love that, but Helen may feel differently. There was some truth to that statement. It was evident Elena was special to them, and they to her.

Jean and Tonya celebrated their birthdays together because their birthdays were just a few days apart. Their 6th and 7th birthday party were princess themed. They both hated it. The decorations were lovely, very girly, and they usually got the same presents, just a bit different. Same doll, different color hair, same dress, different color. Helen believed they wouldn't fight if they were getting the same gifts. She thought wrong. They argued over everything. The two were a bit miffed because they asked for makeup and only got lip gloss. Any attempt at generosity to the two was met with displeasure even anger from them as if they didn't want to be happy.

Artie told Helen not to try so hard and don't spend so much money, that she was only spoiling them there were two other children in the house who ask for nothing and appreciate everything. He would be on the verge of anger and her on the verge of tears when the two spoke of Tonya and Jean. She tried far too hard to make them good and it pained her to see they were always difficult.

Birthday celebrations were never too elaborate after the disappointing princess themed birthday party for the two girls and Artie's talk with Helen about over-spending and spoiling them.

Elena's birthday was in July. She was turning 5, that's a big deal for a child. Five is almost a grown up. Going to school, doing the "big kid" stuff like learning and reading was exciting to Elena. Grandma and Grandpa bought her an apron that made the two girls laugh at her, but to Elena it was one of the most precious gifts she could have gotten.

Helen bought Elena a few books for her birthday which was cause for the two to laugh once more not understanding that Elena truly appreciated her gifts. Elena was able to read some books, Matteo always helped her to read, he taught her the alphabet when she was just two, then would show her words and how to sound them out which she picked up very quickly. The two wanted makeup, toys, and clothes for their birthdays not stupid books.

After a few days of not being able to find her birthday books Helen found them torn up and stuffed in the trash. Helen never told anyone about the books, she knew it was the two girls that Elena's books were ruined. She quietly replaced them and told Elena she found them in the hall closet and was going to keep the books in Matteo's room, so they don't get lost again and since she likes to read with him it was a great place to keep all her books. Matteo knew why they were being kept there – for safe keeping from the two. Her apron was kept at grandma's house for when she went over there with her daddy so she wouldn't get dirty when helping grandma to cook.

Elena continued with her reading, she read through all her birthday books all by herself, so Matteo gave her some big kid books to read. There were a few words that she couldn't sound out or understand and those were the ones that he helped her with while making Elena call him "teacher." She thought it was funny and proudly called him "sir teacher". She was a sponge, wanting to absorb all the knowledge Matteo had, he was a big kid and so smart. She hoped to be as smart as him one day.

Elena would be going to school and couldn't visit with Grandma and Grandpa as much as she or they would have liked. Artie made it a point to take her over on the weekends and even before greeting them Elena had a habit of running to grab her apron from grandma's closet. Once grandpa hid in the closet and scared her so much, she almost tinkled. Her habit quickly changed now upon arriving she made certain to greet her grandparents then cautiously open the closet reaching in ever so slowly to retrieve her apron. They always cooked at Grandma's and Elena was learning to make bread. Artie bought everything they would need to make several loaves of bread, knowing Helen would love to have fresh baked bread for dinner. Helen thought Elena was too young to learn to make something so difficult but with grandma's help the breads were baked to perfection.

Matteo's 10th birthday was coming up, he told Elena she needed to learn how to bake a cake. He wanted a chocolate cake with white frosting and chocolate chips. Elena couldn't make a cake without help, so Helen made the cake and let Elena frost it. It wasn't the prettiest cake, but it was yummy.

Birthdays were a great excuse to have cake and play, gifts were a bonus. On Matteo's 10th birthday, he got the best present ever! A puppy!

The puppy was, according to Artie, "A full-blooded German Shepherd" his buddy knew a guy that found a litter of purebred pups. His friends were great at finding whatever you needed or wanted, Artie always "knew a guy". The pup's huge floppy ears, large paws and dark face would melt anyone's heart. Matteo was so excited he cried, this was the first time Elena saw her brother cry and she began to cry as well. And of course, the two girls laughed at Matteo and Elena calling them "big babies".

Their comments were ignored as Artie chimed in "What are you going to name your pup?" Elena insisted "Biscuit" was the perfect name, it was Matteo's dog so he had the naming rights and named the precious pooch "Champ".

Although Matteo requested the chocolate cake with white frosting and chocolate chips, he was too excited about Champ and didn't want to come back inside the house he was too busy playing with his new friend. Elena brought out some of her doll clothes to put on Champ who cooperated for the most part as Matteo laughed and told her that she can't put girl clothes on his dog. Elena and Matteo sat on the lawn with Champ and took turns cuddling him between running and being chased by the pup. Tonya and Jean were happy to eat more than their share of the cake, so at least it didn't go to waste.

Artie bought a crate for Champ, but Matteo insisted he would wake up to take the puppy outside and promised he wouldn't make a mess. It was his birthday, so Artie agreed. Matteo kept his word, and the puppy didn't make a mess anywhere luckily the crate was never needed. Champ was easily trained, a great guard dog and a gentle companion to all the family.

Matteo taught Champ all the basic commands including paw, sit, down, and fetch. Playing with a ball was Champ's favorite. With some convincing and tugging most of the times he would give the ball back. Matteo and Elena would play with Champ for hours. Champ slept in Matteo's room every night to the dismay of Elena who wanted to snuggle with Champ too. He was a perfect dog. Matteo would joke he finally had a "brother" and was happy his puppy grew too big for Elena's doll clothes.

Artie and Helen had a three-bedroom home on 7 acres of wooded property. There were many secret places to find in the woods Elena and Matteo loved being outdoors. Matteo and his friends built a tree fort, it was kind of shaky but if you were careful, it was fun. They would carry a nervous Champ up to the fort so he could enjoy the scenery as well. The neighbor boys helped Matteo to make a harness to lower Champ back to the ground.

After reinforcing the fort with leftover wood from a neighbor's new garage, Champ learned to like it and would run up to the steps waiting to be carried up then quickly wanted to be lowered in the harness. He was a silly little dog that all the neighborhood kids loved. Beyond the thick wooded area there were cliffs that were about 15 feet tall and stupidly the kids would take the vines from the trees and swing off the cliff then back again as Champ looked on with a furrowed brow, looking concerned.

There were a lot of kids in the neighborhood, mostly boys they were always in Artie's yard because it was the most interesting – with all the woods, and places to explore. Artie loved having kids over his house watching them all play and laugh. Elena made quick friends with David. David was more pretty than handsome.

David's dark blonde hair was never combed and when it grew too long it would curl around his ears. His eyes were blue, a deep dark blue, he was just a few months older than Elena, but everyone thought he was much older because he was so much taller. David started coming over after dinner most days there was always something to do. Just being outside with her friend was enough for Elena. David was kind and made her laugh with all his silly antics and stories about his big brothers.

Matteo and Elena were always outside. Matteo would mow lawns, shovel driveways, and weed gardens to earn money. He saved up quite a bit and having a few hundred acres of undeveloped property behind Artie and Helen's made a great argument for Matteo to get a dirt bike. Artie "knew a guy" of course, his buddy got a dirt bike at a great price. Helen insisted on a helmet, Matteo agreed to always wear the helmet and was thankful he didn't have to wear the elbow and knee pads she bought. Matteo and his buddies were quick to learn how to handle the dirt bike and Matteo was nice enough to share with his friends.

Weekends Matteo and his friends would take hours cleaning his dirt bike making sure that everything was perfect. That clean bike never stayed clean for long, it was odd that they would spend so much time cleaning it to just get it filthy in a matter of minutes.

After the bike was perfectly clean, they would be gone for most of the day taking Champ along with them for "protection". Matteo gave Champ a very slow ride on the dirt bike as the other boys cheered. Champ didn't look too cheerful and was happy to leap off the bike when it stopped.

You could hear the distant hum of the muffler and as they got closer to the house the laughter and whoops from the boys gradually became louder. They made small ramps and mounds to ride the bike over.

Tonya and Jean rarely went outdoors. Elena and her friend David were always playing in the woods catching frogs, chipmunks, all sorts of creepy crawly things, making sure Champ wouldn't eat any of the gross bugs. Watching the big boys on the dirt bike with an occasional ride from Matteo or David's brothers, whenever the big kids included them, it was special.

Helen wouldn't let Elena go into the woods by herself, when David was around it was okay if Champ went with them too, her reasoning was "safety in numbers" which was a good rule to follow. Their house is where you would find most of the neighborhood kids. It was the safe house on the street, the fun house on the street.

Weekends and summers were the best. Chores done early and just exploring all day into the night. Catching lightning bugs putting them in a jar but just for a few minutes then setting them free at once to watch them light up the sky, it was magical. There was always something new to enjoy in the woods. Picnics in the fort, camping out, playing tag, baseball anything outdoors was a good time, and of course the dirt bike. They boys never tired of riding that dirt bike.

When not on his dirt bike, Matteo was always with Champ. One of their favorite things to do was to explore the woods. Matteo and Elena took Champ for a walk into the wooded area where they would inspect and find treasures. Champ dug up a large rock that was loaded with sparkles and Matteo said it was a gift for Elena from him and Champ. She treasured that rock and displayed it proudly on her small dresser it was pretty a faded pink shade with the lovely sparkles it was probably worth a million dollars! Or it was just a rock. Champ loved digging up treasures, huge sticks and would strut with the largest stick – more like small trees - with pride.

Champ was easy to love, his big floppy ears, paws that were too big for his little frame and a tail that wagged for days. Yet there may have never been a time that Jean or Tonya ever pet Champ. Quite possibly the sweetest dog in the world and deserving of all the love. Doubtful Champ ever noticed, he received mounds of attention from Matteo and Elena.

Champ found his favorite spot - under the kitchen table during mealtime right by Elena's feet. She was so good at sneaking Champ chicken gizzards and so thankful Champ was there to gobble up the evidence in silence. One of Helen's go-to meals was rice and gizzards and the smell of it was so repulsive to Elena, but everyone had to eat the dinner that was provided whether you liked it didn't matter. Matteo hated beef stroganoff, so on days Helen made that dinner Champ knew to maneuver over to Matteo's feet.

Elena told Matteo when she's a grownup she's never going to make chicken gizzards, he told her to never make beef stroganoff either just make bread and pasta. Bread and pasta were a favorite, there were so many possibilities when it came to creating new pasta dishes, and bread could be made a million different ways. She agreed that's all she would make.

Most of the food Helen cooked was good, even if it weren't, the family had to eat what was served. Elena didn't grasp why she would have to eat food she didn't like, why make someone eat something that makes them sick? She wanted to cook more but she wasn't allowed to cook without her grandma or her dad helping her. A quick call to grandma would warrant a weekend visit to cook with Elena.

Elena cherished her time with her grandmother cooking, baking, and learning more intricate recipes. She would read to her grandpa who feigned astonishment by the big words she knew. It was comical to watch as her grandparents spoke little English but seemed to understand every sentence Elena read.

Aside from her family, her love of cooking and reading, her friends and Champ rounded out her happiness. Champ was more like one of the kids than a pet, always with Matteo and Elena and their friends playing, sleeping, eating, and missing them when they weren't home.

Matteo would hop on his dirt bike Champ and Elena would chase after him, Champ came close to catching Matteo on several occasions he probably could have caught Matteo if he had wanted. Elena brought out her sparkle rock every chance she had and showed it off to all the kids who, she believed, were truly impressed taking turns holding it and examining the sparkles. They asked Champ to go dig them one up too. He didn't, but they loved him, nonetheless. He was quickly becoming the neighborhood pet.

Artie's buddy gave him a few tents so the kids could enjoy sleeping outdoors in the summer months, he assured Helen, he got them at a great price because he "knew a guy" that bought too many. The neighborhood kids, Elena, Matteo and Champ would make great use of the tents, it became a weekend ritual in the summer months if the tents were up kids would just show up with their sleeping bags.

Artie's bon fires were legendary always much larger than necessary as he encouraged the kids to throw more sticks and wood into the fire pit. It wasn't quite dark outside so the kids gathered up all their goodies and readied the area for their campout. Marshmallows and hot dogs, not even close to being a healthy dinner, weekends were about fun, not nutrition Artie would tell Helen. Jean and Tonya thought camping was gross and wouldn't join the kids. Helen did her best to encourage them to make friends and go outdoors, the closet she could get them outside was to open the windows and allow the breeze to blow through the house.

The two would stay inside eating ice cream while secretly spying on the kids outside, watching through the bedroom curtains to see if they were doing anything bad, they could report back to Helen. Tonya keeping a strict eye on David, hating him for being friends with Elena and not her. Not that she truly wanted a friend, in her jealous mind it was more important for him to like her not Elena.

Some of the neighborhood parents would come over for camp night, sit around the fire while the kids played and just before bedtime, they'd head home leaving the kids and Artie to sleep in the tents. And Champ of course.

Now being a nice hot summer day, Artie didn't quite think his plan through. The grass was quite dry and as the fire grew a spark or two hit the lawn and the lawn caught fire!

If not for the scary part, it was quite comical. Artie grabbed the hose which didn't quite reach, the kids got their blankets and were smacking the flames down then David's dad came over with a shovel and started hitting a few of the flames as some of the parents were just stomping on the flames and laughing and the absurdity of the lawn being on fire.

A short time later the burning grass was smothered. Everyone was laughing and talking about how quick they were to respond, and they should join the volunteer firefighters. The parents brought over fresh blankets, David's dad went home and brought back a couple of beers for him and Artie. The two men were always very friendly, didn't get together often, but when they did, they would talk for hours.

After the lawn fire Artie built a large brick fire pit so he can still have fires that were always bigger than necessary, but they were safer now. The man was always doing something, skilled in so many trades always helping the neighbors with their projects too. He was the neighborhood handyman eager to help anyone in need. Matteo would follow in his father's footsteps; he too was always lending a helping hand to his friends with whatever they needed.

If Jean and Tonya availed themselves to the neighborhood kids, it's quite possible they would have had a great time as well. Kids didn't care what you looked like, they were all about having fun, being silly, being kids. Tonya would talk ill about David every chance she had but only because she had a crush on him and it wasn't reciprocated, he was a very good-looking boy so of course she had a crush on him.

David came over and was waiting for Elena to get her tennis shoes from her room when Tonya showed up in the kitchen and told him she wanted him to be her boyfriend he did his best to politely decline. Her persistence was annoying and when she forcibly tried to kiss him, he said "No! I don't like you!" He didn't say it to be mean, he tried several times to be nice when turning down her unwelcomed advances. Sweet David was incapable of lying, ask him a question, you'll get the truth. She was furious that he embarrassed her like that but couldn't react because right then is when Elena appeared with her shoes.

David told Elena he'll see her outside which was weird because normally they'd grab a bottle of water or Kool-Aid then head out. When she went outside David told her what happened she was so sorry that Tonya tried to kiss her friend and apologized for her behavior. David told her never to apologize for what someone else does and assured her it wasn't a big deal, he just wanted her to know why Tonya was mad.

David was over most days if the weather was uncooperative, he and Elena would be playing a board game or cards at the kitchen table. Since he told her in no uncertain terms that he didn't like her, Tonya would go out of her way to do something to annoy him whether she shoved his chair, pushed him, anything to show her displeasure with him being around Elena. Being outside was an easy way to avoid Tonya because she hated going outdoors.

For Elena and David being outside was always better than being in the house even if it was just lying in the grass examining the blades and searching for new species of bugs that no one knew existed. Champ was running around outside the moment he spotted the kids he ran over and pounced on Elena much to her delight. David play-wrestled Champ to save Elena from the 'monster' dog. Elena told David Champ's birthday was coming up and they should do something special for him. David covered Champs ears and said "shh let's keep it a secret and don't invite Tonya" then they laughed.

Always looking to celebrate something, maybe an excuse for more cake Elena told Matteo they should have a birthday party for Champ's third birthday. This "purebred German Shepherd" still had ears bigger than his head, paws that looked like boots, and he weighed about 50 pounds. Okay, not all of Artie's buddies came through with exactly what Artie asked for, but no one cared, Champ was perfect. Such a sweet goofy looking dog.

Matteo thought it was silly but told her if she wanted to, he was sure Champ would love it. Helen helped Elena to make pumpkin biscuits from a recipe that Grandma gave to Elena. They were sure to save a few for Artie. Jean and Tonya were invited to the party but thankfully they said it was a stupid idea to give a dog a party adding Elena should be in trouble for wasting food on a dog then preceded to consume far more than their fair share of the treats before Champ had even had one. The two girls always made sure to take even if they didn't want or need.

David came over with a gift for Champ – a huge stick. It was funny and probably the highlight of Champ's day. Matteo bought Champ a dog collar that had spikes on it, they were fake spikes that Matteo said would make Champ look "bad ass" Elena gasped at Matteo for swearing and he joked "don't tell mom!". With a candle in the pumpkin biscuit, they sang happy birthday to Champ, Matteo blew out the candle just before Champ chomped the biscuit and swallowed it whole even the candle. Matteo put the new collar on the birthday dog then Champ ran off with his precious new stick.

David and Elena went inside to enjoy some of Champ's birthday cookies. Tonya, although she didn't want to be at the party, strutted by far too many times in an obvious attempt to annoy David. As she passed by for the umpteenth time, she let out a squeaky fart. The laughter that followed could be heard around the block.

If humiliation were within her realm of emotion this may have been what Tonya was feeling as she slapped David on the back and attempted to blame Champ - who was outside with the large stick David have given him.

This made the two laugh even louder causing Tonya to storm off and slam her bedroom door twice because the first slam was muffled by her dirty clothes getting stuck in the doorway. David imitated the fart noise, and they laughed so hard Elena's stomach was cramping. Jean not knowing what just transpired went to the room and as the door opened hollered "what stinks?!" Apparently, Tonya was having tummy troubles and her gas passing troubles continued. David and Elena couldn't handle any more of the painful laughter and had to go outside.

When Artie came home, he was sure to wish Champ a happy birthday and enjoy a pumpkin biscuit with the birthday dog even though Tonya and Jean tried to deter anyone from eating what they insisted was dog food, probably so they could eat them all they were shoveling them in their ugly faces all day. They were pumpkin cookies not dog food and they were delicious. Maybe that's what made her so gassy.

A few days later Tonya stayed home from school, yet another "sick" day. The two were always scheming trying to get out of everything from chores, school, even going to see the grandparents. At some point Tonya miraculously felt better and decided to go outside.

Helen was stunned and pleased to see her outside hoping the fresh air will do her good. Shockingly she even took Champ with her saying he looked like he had to poop so she was going to take him for a walk. Helen fixed a quick lunch then gathered up all the dirty laundry from Tonya's room. The three girls shared same bedroom, but Tonya was the one that would leave filthy clothes all over the room rather than put them in the hamper or take them to the laundry room.

After taking care of some laundry Helen went to the living room to clear up her lunch dishes while enjoying the peace and quiet as Tonya was still outside. She thought to herself how nice this was that Tonya was outside and spending time with Champ, she smiled thinking about how Tonya exhibited some kindness and interest in Champ and being outdoors. As Helen was cleaning up the lunch dishes, she looked out the kitchen window to see Tonya dragging Champ behind her. She noticed Tonya took the new collar off the dog and had Champ on a leash, the leash was wrapped around his neck as a makeshift collar with the leash extending so she can hold the loop of the leash. She was just dragging him from the backyard his body was limp. Helen ran out the door screaming at the top of her lungs for Tonya to let Champ go. Helen was running at full speed yet seemed as if she was standing still.

As Helen reached Champ, she was shocked to see his lifeless body. Tonya matter-of-factly stated "he's dead probably those stupid pumpkin biscuits" no emotion, no concern, no sadness. Helen swung around and met Tonya's face with shocking slap, the slap was hard, eerily loud leaving an instant print across her ugly face.

This was the first time Helen had struck Tonya who didn't react just walked off leaving Helen to cry over Champ's body. Helen carried Champ to the house and lay him on the patio. She went into the house and grabbed one of her newly crocheted blankets and wrapped him gently as her tears fell onto his floppy ears. Assessing what just happened attempting to change the scenario of Tonya's demeanor and struggling to make sense of the leash and no collar. Too many thoughts were spinning through her mind as she broke down crying hysterically over Champ.

Helen called Artie and asked him to come home trying to find the words to say Champ had died. She doesn't know what she said, didn't even remember hanging up the phone she found herself back on the patio cradling Champ. Artie quickly arrived at home, looked at Tonya and asked, "What happened?!" she coldly responded, "The dog is dead" and walked off.

Disgusted by her cold response Artie was steaming inside, overcome with anger. Noticing the handprint on her face he knew it was bad if Helen had smacked the brat. Artie ran to the patio and hugged Helen knowing the pain she was going through and could only imagine what Tonya could have done to earn a handprint.

He asked no more questions, he had more important things to do as he prepared a large hole near the wooded area to bury their beloved pet. Artie choked up looking at the sweet dog, couldn't believe that the little guy was gone. Helen brought him out the collar without telling him that Champ wasn't wearing it when he died.

Artie put the collar in his pocket to save for Matteo. As he threw the dirt from what would be Champ's final resting place Artie cried, he cried not just for Champ, but for the sadness that Elena and Matteo were about to endure, for the sense of evil he felt enveloped Tonya, he prayed, praying for comfort for his children, praying Champ didn't suffer.

Artie dried his tears regained his composure and pet Champ for what would never be long enough. Wondering how to gather the words to explain this loss to the kids. The senseless, painful loss.

Artie had to wait for Matteo and Elena to come home from school knowing they would want to say their goodbyes to their friend. This was the most heartbreaking thing to ever happen to

Matteo and Elena there are no words that would offer comfort. They were so overcome by sadness and were crying uncontrollably. Jean muttered "Bye dog" then went into the house.

Artie did his best to console Champ's friends, as he hugged them, he looked up and there was Tonya and now Jean in the kitchen window they appeared to almost be laughing at the sight of their pain. Artie yelled for Helen to get the girls to bed. They hadn't even had dinner yet, but Artie didn't want to see their glib faces. His anger was getting the best of him, he was furious not only by the behavior of the two girls, but the fact that Champ was a healthy, happy dog that morning. Artie didn't have the answers to Matteo's "Why?"

Helen hadn't said a word to Tonya and was still in shock by what she saw and the look of satisfaction on Tonya's face, she hurriedly had the two girls eat dinner while Artie, Matteo and Elena buried Champ. Matteo put the collar with him, saying it was a gift for Champ and he wanted Champ to keep it Artie tenderly placed the collar around Champ's neck as they all cried.

Lucky for the two girls they were in bed before Artie came back to the house. Matteo and Elena didn't eat dinner, they were just too sad. This was the first time Artie said it was okay for them to skip dinner. Elena slept in Matteo's room that night as they shared stories about Champ. Elena called David in the morning and told him about Champ as she paused through the tears that choked her voice it took her several attempts to explain Champ was gone. Hours later David came over with a sympathy card and a small stuffed German shepherd toy for Elena.

David was a good friend and he loved Champ too. As Elena thanked David, he told her she should put it with the rock Champ got for her. She quickly ran to her room half-expecting it to be gone. Snatching up the beautiful rock she and David decided it would be best to hide the rock where no one else could get to it. She didn't want to risk anything happening to her special rock. She asked Matteo to hide it up in the tree fort, he told her that was a good idea as neither of them trusted Jean nor Tonya they knew she loved that sparkly rock.

The three of them went to the tree fort, dusted off a corner where Elena lay a pillowcase. They placed the rock on top of the pillowcase then the stuffed toy on top of the rock. Matteo said he would get a photo of Champ to put with the display so Champ will always be able to watch over them. They cried for a while, laughed for a bit then headed down the tree talking about the times they carried Champ up to the fort and how much he loved to play. Matteo made steps that he nailed to the tree to get into the fort, and they also added a big rope to swing from. Matteo carved Champ's name into one of the steps, David said he would bring over paint and they can make it super cool.

David's brothers came over and went into the fort yelling down to Elena who was playing in the back with David that the rock was the coolest thing they've ever seen. She smiled in agreement. They had posters of pretty girls and cool cars hanging on the walls and now the sparkly rock.

Matteo went up into the fort to hang out with his friends and Elena and David went exploring. Part of the wooded area was known as the orchard, there were apple, pear, plum and peach trees along with blackberry and raspberry bushes. The two decided to enjoy a snack so David climbed up the pear tree to get the two best pears. Being able to grab a snack right off the trees was an underrated luxury. David joked if Tonya knew how much food there was outside, she'd live outdoors.

When the fruit was ripe enough Artie would put David and Elena in the bucket of a backhoe to get the apples, pears, and other fruits from the tops of the trees. They would compete over who could pick the most. Artie would pay them fifty cents for each bag of fruit they picked. The fruit that fell to the ground was usually left for the wildlife to enjoy.

The neighbors all benefitted from the trees there was enough fruit to share with several families. Artie's mom would jar the peaches and plums to keep in Artie's fruit cellar to enjoy year-round she taught Elena how to jar the food during one of her weekend visits. It was an odd thing to be able to put fresh fruit and vegetables into a jar and eat it months later and it still tasted fresh. Again, like magic.

The fruit cellar was always packed with jarred goodies from Artie's orchard and garden. Tomatoes, peppers, pickles, anything that could be jarred and stored found its way into the cellar.

Artie was great with plants and trees, he worked for the city for many years and worked his way up to a position as the chief horticulturist. He had an 8th grade education but worked hard, never missed a day of work, and knew everything there was to know about every plant. If he wasn't working, tending to his own garden, trees, and yard he could be found pruning the neighbors' trees and shrubs.

He planted hearty shrubs on top of Champ's grave where little bunnies made their home. It was a beautiful spot and Champ would have loved the bunnies, he never hurt any other animal, he would sniff and jump back as if he wanted to play, always gentle, always playful. Elena would take apple slices and carrots to the area hoping they would stay with Champ so he wouldn't be lonely. She and David would spend time in the tree fort admiring that still sparkling rock and stuffed toy. Talking about Champ was still sad, but they didn't cry too much anymore. Their sadness became more of a memory of the love they had for their precious pet.

It broke Artie's heart to not get another dog knowing how much love Matteo and Elena had for Champ. As much as Artie too loved having a dog in the house, he worried about getting another pet. There was something… he just couldn't put his finger on it, there was something about Tonya that almost scared him, she couldn't be trusted.

He knew it wasn't fair to Matteo and Elena to not have a pet since they adored and took such great care of Champ, but something just told him he couldn't get another pet. As the years passed, he encouraged the kids to play in the woods and spot the deer in the pasture, the bunnies and the birds and told them those were their "wild" pets. Buying feed to put in the woods for the animals to enjoy. These were animals that would never be bothered by the two bitches.

Elena, David, and Matteo often visited Champ and the bunnies. It was comforting to see such a nice spot, beautiful plants, and the wildlife that stayed by Champ. Artie knew what plants attracted the wildlife, so he kept them plentiful around the back of the property and all-around Champ's grave.

The two trolls never left the house but for school. Helen enrolled both Jean and Tonya in a sewing class, cooking classes, dance classes, hoping this would make them more well-rounded and ladylike. It didn't work. Neither had any desire in bettering themselves. Helen asked them what they were interested in, if there was something they'd like to learn or a special class they would like to take. They claimed they didn't want to do anything; they were too busy.

Helen thought maybe they didn't want to cook because Elena was so good at cooking, and they didn't want to compete with her. They were always invited to their grandmother's house to cook with Elena, but they always refused. She begged the girls to spend time doing something creative, something crafty, a sport, anything. They were able to entertain themselves doing whatever in their room together telling stories, who knows. Not that anyone complained because not having them around was so peaceful.

Matteo played football, went to a vocational school, and spent very little time at the public school. Matteo was smart, had a lot of friends, very handsome so of course, popular with the girls. He'd go on dates every now and again but couldn't wait to get his license so he could go on a 'real' date and not have his mom drive him to meet a girl. He had the pick of any girl he wanted, he would say "Quality over quantity" was the most important to him and he wasn't going to date a girl just to date a girl. He was a good person, treated others kindly and treated girls like ladies just like Artie taught him.

Going to vocational school saved him from the embarrassment of his two sisters and their damaging reputations. The two hadn't absorbed any life lessons from Helen or Artie, never tempted to do right, to be good. It was odd they were never willing to better themselves. Lacking the moral compass to feel for others or to feel embarrassment for their atrocious behavior was stupefying.

Jean had to repeat the fifth grade and ended up in the same classes as Tonya. Which worked out well since making friends wasn't their strong suit. They didn't want to have friends, not having the qualities to be a friend limited their desires to make friends. They talked ill of every other girl, finding fault in anything. Jean put on a tough girl act trying to frighten the other girls with the help of Tonya telling lies about how Jean beat up 3 girls and broke a girl's arm this was their way of preventing retaliation or stopping girls from commenting back about Jean's huge nose or about Tonya being fat. Not a way to make friends, but a way to solidify a shitty reputation.

At thirteen Jean's body grew much quicker than her mind. Jean loved to use her assets to tease any young hormone driven boy or sick man who would give her the slightest attention. Jean was known around the school as the "fun" girl and took her role as school slut seriously. She was certain all the boys had their turn. Generous to a fault. It's not fair to say "all the boys" there were boys smart enough to be selective and not want some skank no matter how easy she was. But the boys who were willing were plentiful which would make one consider the words of Matteo "quality over quantity" the boys that found their way between her filthy legs were repulsive in their own right.

Tonya, trying to compete with Jean, was growing in all the wrong places. Tonya was quite portly; however, the boobs just weren't there. Why does any girl think putting tissue paper in their bra is a good idea? So, there was Tonya stuffing the tissues in her bra in a poor attempt to get the interest of the boys. Any boy. Sadly, the boys would tease Tonya by calling her "TON Yeah!" She acted as though she wasn't hurt by their comments. Any 12-year-old girl would be affected by the horrible teasing of their peers, especially the boys.

Helen tried to help her lose weight by serving healthier options for dinner packing extra vegetables in her lunch, but nothing worked. Tonya acted as though she didn't care about being hefty making no effort to stop at two slices of cake or enjoy a family sized bag of chips. Helen did her best to not buy the junk food, but Tonya cried and threw a fit if she was without her snacks.

Jean liked that she was prettier than Tonya, pretty in a 'not fat' way. Her looks left a lot to be desired. Her large nose, freckled face and cow breath were only overlooked because of her big boobs. That won't last too long. Eventually other girls in the school will blossom then Jean will have to rely on her personality and if that is to be the case, she will be sorely lacking. Jean continued with her conquests; she had a few regulars that gave her enough attention to dupe her into believing she was desirable.

Teen boys can be quite conniving when their hormones kick in. They knew just what to say to get their "good time" with Tonya. The word got out quickly - tell the fat one she's pretty and you'll be sure to get a blowjob. Tell the big boobed one "hello" and you'll get anything and everything. The teasing of "TON Yeah" didn't last too long, as soon as the boys figured out it was to their benefit to be a bit nice to her. Surely Tonya knew that she was being used, somehow, she didn't seem to care. She was getting attention of the boys that was her goal.

Can't say this enough…Matteo's "quality over quantity" mantra would have served these two well.

The two girls were so wrapped up in their own adventures, desires, and scummy boys they had little room to be bothered by issues that didn't involve the two of them. Tunnel-vision was their downfall. They couldn't focus on more than one task at a time, at this time it was boys.

The girls came home from school and headed to their room to select their outfits for the following school day. Elena was at the kitchen table doing homework, Matteo just got back from his friend's house and Helen was getting dinner prepared.

Artie came home and was visibly upset. He took Helen into the bedroom, after a few moments Helen could be heard sobbing. Something was wrong. As Artie gathered the children into the living room he explained his parents, grandma, and grandpa, have died. His words cracked and his voice was just barely above a whisper. There was a confusion and disbelief about him the sadness was overwhelming.

Matteo and Elena immediately burst into tears hugging Artie and Helen. It would be different for Jean and Tonya they weren't close to family members – cousins, aunts, grandparents...they showed no affection or happiness when anyone visited. Always turning down invitations to go to their grandparents' home with Elena, they would go to birthday celebrations or events Helen dragged the kids to but would gravitate toward one another and just go off by themselves.

Jean and Tonya whimpered and made crying noises, but it wasn't real. Artie's parents were the only grandparents they knew, Helen's parents died when Matteo was a baby, so they didn't know the other grandparents. How could they not be affected by this massive loss? Grandma would cook with Elena and braid her hair, she was an expert braider, Grandpa taught Matteo how to make salami and wine – claimed he never let Matteo sip that wine, but Artie knew better. They were amazing grandparents and will be missed so massively.

Artie's sisters came over the house about an hour after Artie told the children. Aunts Maria and Giana's husbands comforted them as they cried. Everyone hugged and consoled one another and as the adults gathered around the kitchen table the children were told to go to the living room. Artie's tone changed a bit he was louder almost angry. The sisters hugged and calmed him. They all prayed then talked about what happened.

Jean and Tonya went on about their business, Matteo and Elena stood closely to the kitchen in hopes to get some answers. Turns out the grandparents were killed by a drunk driver, so their dad had every right to be furious, it was a senseless way to die they were too good to die. Just driving to the market in the middle of the afternoon to pick up dinner and now they're dead. A drunk driver. Middle of the day. The pain in Artie's eyes, the anger, the disbelief, it was unbearable. Elena began to cry, and Matteo took her to his room.

Artie saw they were listening and heard what happened, he went to Matteo's bedroom, sat down and explained to the two of them in a more gentle way than the conversation he had with his sisters. He quelled his anger and talked about how loved they were, and that grandma and grandpa thought the world of them. Maria and Giana soon joined Artie and they talked for quite some time as they offered comfort to Elena, Matteo, and one another. The crying subsided and stories about the grandparents were plentiful. It was nice to have family to help through times like this.

Artie was determined that the drunk driver be sent to jail. Several of Artie's friends assured him that they would take care of the situation. He had so many friends, they were like family, enjoyed spending time at the Italian clubs while enjoying fresh salami, wine and the best cheeses. They all knew someone who knew someone who knew a guy. With all his friends there was never a problem that couldn't be handled. That was the last anyone heard about the drunk driver. Artie never asked, or maybe he did, he just never shared what happened.

The day of the funerals was beautiful. Sunny with a spattering of soft clouds. Artie and his sisters took care of all the details. From what Elena could remember, the service was beautiful. Grandma and Grandpa were placed in a mausoleum. It was stunning but the touch of the marble was cold, and Elena hoped they would be comfortable, Artie assured her they loved their resting place. Matteo held Elena's hand throughout the day as Jean and Tonya mocked them calling them boyfriend and girlfriend. Their lack of compassion was expected but still disturbing. Helen often reminded them why they were there and told them to "straighten up".

Artie stayed home for a few days from work. He was quiet. It was odd to see their dad like this, it hurt to see he was in pain. Elena did what she did best, she cooked for him making some of his favorite treats that grandma had taught her, although Artie felt he couldn't eat, he was so pleased by the gesture he ate everything Elena brought to show his appreciation. Matteo sat with his dad, so Elena brought him a plate of food as well. Normally they weren't allowed to eat in the living room, but this time it was okay.

Helen plated up dinners for the two girls and took it to their room, it was a treat for them to eat in their bedroom instead of at the kitchen table. The first thought was they wouldn't have to wash dishes so that made them happy. Matteo hung out in the living room sitting on the sofa near Artie If he wanted to talk, Matteo would be there. Helen cleaned up the dinner dishes then sat with Artie and Matteo. Elena sat in Matteo's room for a while to avoid the sisters. The longer she could be away from them, the better. Artie announced "bedtime" the kids knew the routine, brush your teeth, put on your pajamas, say goodnight to mom and dad and get to bed. It was nice to hear Artie say "bedtime" he wasn't saying much, it was just nice to hear his voice.

As Elena entered the bedroom the two were talking. She overhead Tonya ask Jean "Do you think we'll get any money from them dying?" Jean excitedly responded, "I hope so!" Elena came in the room and said, "You are fucking bitches!" grabbed Tonya by her hair and punched her in the back of the head – something she learned from the bitches, it won't leave a mark. Jean was next, Jean scrambled onto her bed twisting and pulling away from Elena's grasp but not before Elena landed a punch to her fat nose. Her big nose began to bleed but it was worth any punishment Elena was about to endure, her fists clenched her eyes seething with anger she was going to continue giving them a beat down.

Unfortunately, their screams brought Helen and Artie to the room. As the door opened Jean ran up incoherently crying about her bleeding nose and Tonya crying about her head hurting so badly from Elena punching her attempting to add Elena swore at them. It was a chaotic scene that brought Matteo to the room as well. Artie looked at Matteo and guided him out of the room because he didn't want Helen to see the two of them laughing. Matteo whispered, "Yay Elena!" as he and Artie exchanged high-fives.

Helen took Jean to the bathroom to clean her bloody nose, got an ice pack for Tonya's head then told them to go back to their room. What? This was awesome. Not that Elena was going to make a habit of calling them fucking bitches, and kicking their asses, in fact it was the first time she's ever yelled at them or hurt them for any of their bullshit, it was so nice to not be punished for something they both deserved.

This really pissed off Jean and Tonya which was another small win for Elena. The wins kept coming, Artie let her sleep on the sofa that night so she didn't have to be in the same room as the two victims. As Elena fixed her blanket on the sofa Matteo walked over and held up her arm and just above a whisper in the hopes the bitches would hear announced "ladies and gentlemen the new champion…" she quickly pulled her arm down so their mom wouldn't think they were making fun of what happened.

Artie gave Elena an approving wink she smiled and lay on the couch to sleep. Thinking about how giving Jean a bloody nose and punching Tonya was so gratifying and maybe even made her dad chuckle a bit made her drift to sleep with a smile on her face.

Jean and Tonya were mad that nothing happened to Elena that she didn't get into any trouble for swearing at them and kicking their asses which they wouldn't fully admit, they convinced one another that they got the best of Elena. However, they would find a way to make her pay for what she did, for now they were happy to miss a few days of school due to their grandparents' untimely death.

They spent most of the days in their room, on the phone and giggling amongst themselves. They came out for meals and to sneak snacks into their bedroom. If they knew Elena had been making the dinners, they may have not scarfed it down so quickly. Elena was almost as good as her grandmother when it came to baking bread, no one noticed, Matteo said it was perfect, but Elena knew there was a slight difference, grandma's was best. The girls would each grab a loaf for themselves so Elena could never make less than 4 loaves at a time. This way the whole family could enjoy some.

Time to go back to school. The bitches were back to their old tricks, trying to gain sympathy for the tragic loss of their grandparents. A few of the teachers gave them a pass on some of their assignments, so it worked. Why anyone gave the two the slightest leeway with their proven track-record of misdeeds was dumbfounding. Elena didn't get a pass, she kept up with all her schoolwork thanks to David bringing over notes from class and any assignments that would be due.

Now to get back to the boys. Using the excuse that "insert boy name here" will make them feel better about their loss if they would have sex with them. The scummy boys were eager to help. The athletes, the boys with good grades, the shy boys, boys who had sisters, they were the ones that didn't care how easy the two were, they had no interest in the "uglies" as some of the boys nick-named the two. Of course, that would lead Jean and Tonya to accuse them of liking boys instead of girls, anything they could throw out hoping some excuse for not being wanted would stick. In their world they were amazing, sexy, and every man/boy should desire them.

Some of the classmates knew Jean and Tonya had a younger sister, but she wouldn't be joining the Middle school until next year. The gross boys figured another sister meant they'll be able to add another notch to their belts, bedposts, whatever the boys were 'notching'. They'd be in for a rude awakening when they learn just how different Elena is from the uglies.

Luckily this was before social media so mom and dad were clueless. Jean and Tonya came home and put on the sweet little schoolgirl act and sadly, it worked. Artie working his city job made it easy for Jean and Tonya to keep the 'good girl' illusion alive or so they thought. No one believed they were "good" just as long as they weren't causing trouble that was the best Helen could ask.

They didn't have to see their dad too often and their mom seemed to have a disinterest in what was going on in their daily lives. Almost as though she had given up. Understandably so, there was no pleasing the two and efforts to bring them any happiness were in vain.

They never showed passion in anything that Helen would suggest or try to teach them she found herself just getting frustrated with them. Why were they so different, what did she do to make them this way? The guilt she felt over their behavior was unfounded. There was nothing she did as a mother to make the two behave the way they do. It was just in them. Something different. No amount of love would change them.

Tell a mother she did nothing wrong. She'll never believe you. Helen just couldn't get through to the two – why was it Elena and Matteo were great kids, and these two, were always miserable for lack of a better term. Artie noticed it early on; he shrugged off their behavior hoping it was a drawn-out phase trying his best to include all of his kids in every adventure. He never forced the two to hang out, camp, play in the yard, he wanted them to want to do it, not be forced to do it. At times he felt guilt too that maybe he should have insisted they join in on the camping nights, cooking at grandma's, he tried hundreds of times to talk to just the two of the girls they would respond with one-word answers, never offering a chance at bonding like a father/daughter should.

He was a great dad and if the two would have given him a chance they would have flourished. As much as Artie worked, he always made time for his kids. The two never made time for him. He'd come home from work and ask about their days, of course they couldn't tell him what they were really up to so they would make up how great they did on a test which no one believed, but it was better than their truth. Dinner was the only time they spent any time with the family, though they ate so quickly sometimes they reminded Elena of Champ, they wouldn't chew their food, just swallow.

After school routines were just so routine. Set the dinner table, put dinner on the table, clear the dishes, wash the dishes, do homework, bath, and bedtime. It was Thursday evening, for some reason Tonya was outside – unusual for her, but a welcome break. Elena was finishing up the dinner dishes and the peace didn't last too long… Tonya came in crying that she hurt herself. Helen asking what happened, Tonya crying through her exaggerated breaths said she fell in the woods. Her arms were all scratched up and she had a small cut on her knee. Damn crybaby. Twelve years old and she acted like she lost a leg.

Helen cleaned up Tonya's boo-boos then it was bedtime. Jean was so kind to help Tonya into bed – helping to create the illusion of serious injury. They played off and encouraged one another's questionable behavior effortlessly. Tonya let out a few moans and 'ows' hoping for attention. Jean was the only one who complied, her own personal Florence Nightingale. Idiots. Elena looked at this as another small victory. Tonya wasn't seriously injured, just a couple of scratches, but her crying made Elena almost smile. The only hope was she'd quit sniveling so they could sleep.

The phone rang, Elena heard her dad say, "What's up Frank?" it was David's dad. Probably wanting to drink beer. Elena heard her dad leave after hanging up the phone, so she was sure that's what they were doing. Drinking beer. She liked that her dad was friends with David's dad.

Jean, Tonya, and Elena shared a bedroom. Elena on the top bunk, Tonya on the bottom bunk (kicking the top bunk continuously) and big-boobed Jean in her own bed. As Jean comforted Tonya and her boo-boos, they were whispering and giggling. They were sure to talk loud enough for Elena to hear, but not too loud – didn't want their parents to hear. Tonya was hoping she wouldn't be permanently scarred, a scar wouldn't deter from her unsightly face it just may enhance her looks. She should be so lucky.

Tonya was looking forward to working her injuries to get attention at school the next day. Jean told her she could probably skip school if she complained to Helen enough. Tonya loved that idea any excuse to miss school was a bonus. Although she'd miss out on possible sympathy from the boys.

They talked about all the boys that "liked" them and how "popular" they were. Jean regretted telling Tonya to try and get out of going to school because she would have no one to hang out with and there was no way Jean could stay home. Jean changed Tonya's mind and talked her into going to school to see the boys. They acted as though the boys were so enthralled with them, which wasn't the case. If they wanted sex, they'd pay the two some attention aside from that there was no conversation or friendship with them.

They let Elena know she would never be as popular as they were, which Elena could not care less about. There was no need to be 'popular' their small minds would disagree; popularity was an important goal. Their behavior towards Elena never waned from when they were toddlers it just became more aggressive, they could be more extreme in their cruelty. Taunting Elena with comments like "I wonder if grandpa and grandma are cold…did you hear a dog bark?" Evil bitches. Sick cold-hearted bitches. Knowing if she reacted to any of their comments it would give them satisfaction and that was not an option.

Elena would put a pillow over her head to deafen their comments and disgusting chats. She counted the days down until Saturday. Saturday mornings were the best, good weather meant David would be coming over and the two would explore the woods and create a world only the two of them knew.

After all the years of playing in the woods, it never got old. David and Elena enjoyed one another's company, they would go to the tree fort and read books, eat lunch whatever they wanted to do. They would climb up the fort that thankfully was improved upon over the last few years and was sturdy now.

Being up in the tree fort you can see above the houses and across the street. Whenever David's dad started yardwork David could be found in the fort trying to avoid helping his dad. Truth be told, if David's dad wanted to find him, he knew where to look. David's dad would joke with Artie that he wasn't going to pay for the wedding. The dads enjoyed that their kids were close, and they were good kids. Who knows…Maybe they will get married in 15 or 20 years.

David had the weekly chore of taking the trash to the curb and bringing the empty cans back to the house. He too had to do dishes and clean up around the house. His older brothers were part of Matteo's "cool group" they were driving now and that was a huge deal in the neighborhood. The older guys liked to compare cars and play mechanic. Open the hoods and look under get a little dirty and act as if they fixed something.

Most of them had girlfriends, the girls would gather around talking, laughing, and tossing their long, beautiful hair in a flirtatious way as the guys bragged about their cars. They were a cool bunch, but David and Elena were too young to hang out with them. Matteo would take them for ice cream it was a way of showing off his car, a car that one of Artie's friends got at "a real good price" that he just couldn't pass up. It was a Mercury Grand Marquis that was just a couple of years old, ran great, very low mileage, not the car Matteo dreamt of having, but he was happy to have any car at this point. The two bitches wouldn't go for ice cream, but Matteo always brought them back a nice treat.

Friday morning Artie's car was still in the driveway, Helen said he was helping a neighbor and he would see them after school. David wasn't in school on Friday, but Elena knew she'd see him the next day and would ask him why he wasn't in school. His mom was cool sometimes she would let him 'cut' school, saying he needed a day with mom. Elena had perfect attendance always believing school was important always wanted to learn what everyone else knew and how they learned it, bordering on annoying.

Elena was certain to take especially good notes so she can share with them with David and help him with the assignments he missed, because there is always that one teacher that loved to load up the weekend homework. David was a good student; he didn't study much he was just smart – even without studying. Elena took full credit saying it was because of her expert note taking.

Coming home from school on Friday she glanced across the street to see if David was outside. His dad was home early so that means David can't come over because his dad knows he didn't go to school. His dad was stricter than this mom and if you were too sick for school, you're too sick to play. Artie brought pizza home for dinner and picked up donuts too. It was going to be a great night for Tonya. Artie didn't eat dinner, he went back over Frank's house, probably to drink more beer, Elena surmised.

Maybe it was the sugar from the donuts, but Tonya just would not shut up at bedtime and kept Elena up most of the night talking to Jean about their usual dumb crap. They talked about what kind of men they plan to marry how they're going to have kids, a mansion, and a maid. Their plans were laughable who would want to marry either of these two beasts?

Saturday morning Elena got out of bed a little later than usual thanks to the two keeping her up late with their idiotic stories. Elena washed up then headed to the kitchen for breakfast. Helen and Artie were in the living room, the television was off, and they were very quiet.

Artie looked up and ran to Elena hugging her tightly all he could say was "I'm so sorry, I'm so sorry". Helen came over and explained David didn't come home Thursday night, he was found last night at the bottom of the cliffs. Her friend was gone. What stupid stuff was Helen saying? This isn't true, David can't be dead. Artie just squeezed Elena in the tightest bearhug she never felt, she was numb.

David. Elena's best friend *was* dead. Matteo didn't' tell Elena that they were searching for David since Thursday night he didn't want to worry her. They all just figured he was doing something dumb like sleeping in the fort or forgot to tell his parents he was sleeping at a buddy's house. Matteo came out of his room and did his best to comfort Elena. Now she understood why David wasn't in school on Friday, and why his dad was home early, and they weren't drinking beer, they were searching for her friend.

Tonya and Jean slept a few more hours, it was nearly noon when they came out of the bedroom. When Helen told them about David, they asked what was for breakfast. Bitches. Artie yelled at them to go back to their rooms and don't come out! Helen made them sandwiches and took them to their room without a word. One would have to question whether the two had some sort of blockage in their brains. To show no compassion or empathy for anyone or anything can't be a normal reaction.

What happened to David? Everyone just assumed David was swinging off the cliffs and fell. Why would he be out there by himself? That was not a "David" thing to do. Then Elena for a passing moment thought about Tonya and her boo-boos, maybe David wasn't alone. No, it's Tonya and David would never hang out with her – he knew she was nasty; he didn't like her and would never hang out with that trash. Stop. She's a horrible beast, David hated her.

Elena wished she were there to stop David from taking chances at the cliffs, they all would swing from the cliffs, yes it was a dumb thing to do, but they only did it when the bigger kids were around. The bigger kids would hang from the vines to make certain they wouldn't break then the younger kids would take turns swinging. The parents never knew that the kids were taking such chances, surely, they would have put a stop to this activity had they known. The kids felt there was no reason to think anything bad was going to happen because they've been doing this for years.

Another funeral. Why so many funerals? Life isn't supposed to be like this, David was a kid. A friend. He was special. To love someone and to lose them carries such an intense, lingering pain, it fades but is always within you. To die in such a stupid way, just playing having fun, doing something they've done for years and now he's dead. It's not fair. It's not right. His mom and dad were surrounded by David's brothers and their friends. So many people came to the funeral, teachers, classmates, neighbors, the line of visitors was down the street. Jean and Tonya were at the funeral and after 30 minutes begged Helen for a ride home. She obliged. She didn't want them there with their unsympathetic behavior on display.

The hardest thing to do was to say goodbye to her sweet friend. Elena was distraught. Matteo and Artie comforted David's parents and Elena. His parents told Elena she meant so much to David and thanked her for being so special to him. That's how they were their son was gone and they consoled Elena. They were great parents. It was such a tragic loss. His brothers were quiet it was obvious from their swollen eyes they had been crying quite a bit they looked so grown up in their suits as they hugged Matteo and they talked quietly. David loved his brothers and bragged about them often he liked talking about how they were going to teach him to shave, drive, everything the cool kids did. Goodbyes are the hardest part of love.

A few weeks after David died, the big kids cut down all the vines so no one else could swing from them. Artie cut down a few of the trees that were too near the cliffs and the older boys and a few of their dads chopped them up into firewood. Artie bought a bunch of boxwood shrubs and David's dad and brothers cleared out the large boulders, rocks and sticks at the bottom of the cliffs. Artie brought truckloads of dirt and filled in the area off the cliffs. The neighborhood kids, Matteo and Elena planted the more than 40 boxwood shrubs along the Cliffside and at the bottom of the cliffs. So IF someone ever fell off the cliff again, hopefully they would land in the shrubs and wouldn't be badly hurt.

Artie's gift of the shrubs helping to make a safe place at the cliffs meant the world to David's family and to Elena. He was a great protector – obviously Matteo got his courage from his father. David's dad and mom were lucky to have their older sons to comfort and help them. They both stepped up and were caring for their parents, especially their mom, she was really distraught for quite some time. The neighbors took turns cooking meals for the family and provided meals that would last a few months. Everything packed up and stored in the garage freezer so the family would have one less thing to worry about. Matteo took over several loaves of bread baked by Elena much to the delight of David's brothers.

Seemingly the only unaffected persons by David's death were Jean and Tonya. Everyone had some great memory of David. Everyone but the bitches helped to clean up the cliffs and plant the shrubs. The two of them were just cold-hearted, self-centered, disgusting bitches. Now that they were a bit older, they weren't home as much. The two would claim they were going to a friend's house, a party, roller skating, anything to get out of the house. A couple of boys would pick them up, Artie wanted to meet them, but the two insisted they were just friends, not boyfriends, and if Artie bothers them, they won't come over anymore. Helen knew they didn't have any friends but welcomed the break from the two.

Nothing much changed for Tonya and Jean they continued to do things and blame Elena. They never let up, nothing was off limits. Their comments about everything that Elena was sad about gave them such pleasure. They had stories about David – they weren't true stories and were told in a higher-than-normal tone to ensure Elena could hear. Elena thought about the time Tonya farted in front of David and laughed out loud, it was uncontrollable laughter. You know you shouldn't be laughing but can't stop. This really pissed off the two. What in the hell was so funny? They were trying to make Elena cry, not laugh! She knew that David made her remember the fart so she would laugh. He would do that. Just like David to make Elena feel better.

David couldn't stand the two, he was never too harsh when talking about them, probably a way to avoid hurting Elena's feelings he should have known she felt the same way. She remembered how angry Tonya was when David said he didn't like her that made her smile too. Elena was stronger than they knew she wouldn't let them see how much they hurt her, quell their satisfaction and hopefully they would stop with their torment. They knew nothing about David, they knew nothing about anyone but themselves. The two continued with their nonsensical plots - so illogical it was hard to understand why anyone would take them seriously. Immaturity at its finest.

Once they claimed they found pills by Elena's purse. Two green pills. They ran to their parents and exclaimed "Elena is on drugs!" This panicked their mother who was quick to believe the pills belonged to Elena. Although the pills more than likely belonged to one of the bitches – probably birth control, there was no sense bothering to explain.

Here comes another unwarranted punishment. Punishments included anything from going to bed right after dinner for a month, being grounded for a month, doing all the chores for a month…yes - Mom had something about punishments having to last a month. That and getting your hair pulled, or hit with a belt, brush, or anything swingable. More than likely just a way for

Helen to take out her frustration over the two misfits and her own perceived failing as a mother.

Helen often used the phrase "Wait until your father gets home!" Poor Artie, working all day then comes home to bullshit created by Jean and Tonya. Although their mom didn't know that - she always believed Elena was to blame or behaved as though she knew Elena was to blame. Guess who dented mom's car? Who broke mom's curio cabinet? How did the bed break? The two even went as far to claim that Elena hit them on several occasions, knowing that Helen knew she hit them when their grandparents died, it was an easy lie to perpetuate.

"Wait until your father gets home" wasn't a threat to Elena. She knew he knew. He was more in-tune to what was going on even in his absence. Again, his street-smarts go a long way. He saw for himself repeatedly how they reacted to sad situations, how unfeeling they were, he stopped short of saying he didn't like them. They were his daughters after all, just not very likeable.

It was beginning to feel as though Helen was trying to win over the affection of the bitches by pretending to believe their claims, stories, bullshit negative comments, whatever, about Elena. This made the bitches smile and Helen felt that was a way to connect to them. To show them she cared for them too.

Artie saw something in Elena. Artie was more observant and watched when the kids were just being kids. He always noticed Jean and Tonya leaving Elena out, he could see they weren't very kind to her and when he tried to discuss this with Helen, she brushed it off saying "You just like her best because she's pretty. She's always doing something bad when you're at work". Helen forced the words blaming Elena for misdeeds and as she heard them, she didn't believe them either. When the sisters weren't around, Elena was a joy. She never witnessed Elena being anything but kind and caring.

Helen reflected on everything she had done for the sisters, taking them to dance, sewing class, girl scouts, etc. and they refused to do any of the activities. She felt badly for never signing up Elena for any classes, she was too busy trying to save the two girls, trying to make them good, Elena was an afterthought. Elena seemed unaffected by the lack of attention from her mother, she had a happy life for the most part. Artie, Matteo, friends, her aunts, cousins and neighbors - they all made life enjoyable.

Artie did favor Elena; she was always ready with a smile or a helping hand. Going to grandma's house to cook with her and learn how to make breads and pastas she was special. Artie showed Elena how to cook some of his favorite dishes and it took off from there. Elena was always in the kitchen and now was tasked with making dinners for the family. When Artie raved about the amazing food Elena created Jean and Tonya would just glare at her. Elena wished dad would just keep his praise to himself, it was just going to cause more problems for Elena when he went to work. Any time they could make her life uncomfortable they would.

While in the kitchen Elena was drinking a glass of water when Tonya came up from behind her and smacked the glass into Elena's face. The glass hit Elena's tooth and chipped it, when Elena shouted "You chipped my tooth!" Tonya began to cry saying "Don't tell, don't tell please don't tell…" Elena had a beautiful smile, she went to Helen to show her the small chip on her tooth Helen very angrily asked "How did this happen?!" Elena didn't tell on Tonya, she claimed she just banged her tooth with the glass herself. A trip to the dentist and everything was fine. It was a very small chip and unnoticeable the dentist quickly filed it down and her smile was perfection once again. Helen always said Elena had the prettiest smile so she may have panicked more than necessary.

Elena had multiple chances to inform her parents of wrongdoings by the two sisters, the abuse they inflicted upon her, the horrible things the two said and did. She kept it to herself not in fear of getting them reprimanded, because to add more proof of their unpleasantness to her parents would be more damaging to them than the bitches.

A few months later things were back to normal. Helen had made the kids breakfast, Tonya insisted on bacon, and if she requested something it was in Helen's best interest to oblige. Getting ready for school the two put on skirts they would be able to hike up higher once they left the house. Elena wore jeans and a tee-shirt always going for comfort over style.

Elena was helping clean the breakfast dishes when Tonya stomped her past grabbing the last few strips of bacon to shove in her face. Then for whatever reason, for no reason, Tonya became angry with Elena and shoved her into the stove. Elena's footing slipped and the pan containing the bacon grease wobbled. Tonya scowled at Elena then tipped the pan of grease onto Elena's hair. Mercifully the grease had cooled enough not to burn Elena but saturated her hair. Tonya leaned over and called her an ugly bitch and said she wished the grease would have burned off her stupid face.

Tonya shoved her way past Helen who was making her way into the kitchen. Seeing Elena with bacon grease all over her hair and dripping onto her shirt Helen cried. She sat down on the floor and cried "she did this to you, didn't she?" Elena responded, "I'm okay, Mom". This was the first day Elena missed school. The two left the house to wait for the bus without saying a word and without their lunches. Helen put baby powder in Elena's hair to absorb the grease then had her lay on the kitchen counter with her head in the sink.

Helen washed Elena's hair more than 6 times each time providing a soothing massage. Helen was sad that Elena put up with so much from the two and astounded by this little girl's strength. After a few hours her hair was clean and beautiful and maybe a little more shiny than usual. The kitchen was clean, and Elena asked if she could make some bread. Helen laughed, this girl and her cooking. Absolutely, fresh bread was always a welcome addition to any meal.

Elena's cooking was appreciated by everyone. Matteo would bring his friends over and ask her to whip something up for them – usually it was an easy pasta dish, and the boys would devour it like they were eating the best meal of their lives. It was an easy way for him to brag about his sister without being so blatant. They all loved Elena's cooking and always helped themselves to more.

Cooking was Elena's peace. She would cook and get into her own world and not have to deal with Jean and Tonya.

Spreading his time between vocational school, his friends and girls, Matteo was home less and less. Boys were allowed much more freedom than girls. It was a thing back then. Being stuck at home with just the bitches was nauseatingly painful. They would try to tease Elena, bully, make fun of her, the usual tactics. There were moments a wave of strength and anger would wash over Elena but would refrain from knocking their faces in, once was enough…it was easier to let them do their damage and move on. Who knows what they would resort to if Elena did retaliate, there was no limit to their evil.

Elena, to a fault, just didn't care. Didn't care that her sisters were bitches. Bitches is a good word for them. There are so many more derogatory words that would describe them, but this will do for now. The two often smacked, hit, even pulled Elena's hair as she passed by them. With their parents out of the house running errands, working, whatever the case, that was their opportunity. Tonya came up from behind and smacked Elena right in the eye just as Matteo walked in the back door.

The two ran to their room and slammed the door, Matteo came in and asked Elena what was going on matter-of-factly she replied "Tonya just hit me in the eye, they didn't want you to go after them" Matteo told Elena to meet him in the bathroom. This was odd. Elena was in the bathroom when Matteo came in with a wine cork and a lighter. He lit the cork, cooled it off then wiped it under Elena's eye to blacken it then told her to pretend cry.

Normally it was best to just to ignore their lame attempts of abuse knowing Helen didn't need any more conflict, issues, or complaints about the two and wouldn't step in to stop their abhorrent behavior.

Messing with them may be more fun especially with Matteo backing her up. Hearing Elena's cries from the bathroom as their dad pulled into the driveway caused Tonya to go into a frenzy, she was outside the bathroom demanding "let me see, let me see!" Matteo briefly opened the door stating, "you're in trouble now, look what you did!" Elena turned around to show her blackened eye. Tonya balled uncontrollably as Jean pointing at Tonya adamantly declared "It was her it was her." Matteo shut the door, Elena cleaned up her face as Tonya and Jean hid in their rooms knowing that when Dad sees Elena's eye they would be in huge trouble. Matteo and Elena laughed so hard, Artie and Helen had no clue what just happened.

Elena was 12 and would be starting middle school in the summer. Middle school is scary. You're going to be around big kids, older kids, will they be nice? Elena figured they wouldn't be nice because the older kids were her bitch sisters. She heard plenty of stories about the boys and how popular her sisters were, so she hoped there would be a chance some of the older kids would be nice to her.

Luckily the middle school was huge. Huge to a 12-year-old. So huge that she only had to see the bitches on the bus ride. The school wasn't too difficult to navigate, there were only a few classroom changes throughout the day. Elena had a lot of friends and they enjoyed school. The teachers were surprisingly nice – after hearing stories from the bitches, Elena was nervous on what to expect. Then there were the boys.

Sitting at the cafeteria table Elena and her friends were enjoying a break from class when a group of boys walked by and did one of those 'cough' talks saying "whore" Elena and her friends shot their disapproving looks at the moronic, immature boys. Times like this Elena really missed David he never acted like a jerk, he was sweet and kind. These boys could have learned a lot about from David.

That was just the start. Did you ever go into a restroom at school and write something on the bathroom stall? So did a lot of other kids.

A quick trip to the restroom can be quite educational. Scrawled in what looked like a fading purple marker "Jean or Tonya? Which one fucked your boyfriend?" That was bad enough. The comments surrounding the question went from bad to worse.

The door was practically covered in whore comments. Now jerk's behavior in the cafeteria made sense.

Elena's reputation was already determined before she stepped foot in the school. Thanks to her trashy sisters. Aside from all the schoolwork Elena needed to work on her reputation. She is not like her sisters. Nothing like her sisters and she was sure it wouldn't take long for everyone to figure that out. Elena had the best group of friends, and they knew that Elena was nothing like her sisters, her sisters were just jerks.

Studying, minding her own business, and staying away from the boys. Sounds like a good plan, but when you're faced with the whore sisters' conquests on the daily it can be very draining. Ignoring the comments, avoiding the boys, just studying. Seemed to work. Having support of her friends and hanging out with them was very uplifting. There were more good girls in school than bad. Unfortunately, it's the few bad ones that ruin it for the rest of the girls. Especially when the bad girls are your sisters.

The scummy boys soon learned Elena was not like her slut sisters and nicknamed her "prude" and "prick tease". If there must be a label, I guess prude is better than whore or slut. So this is the root of their popularity. Sad. Sad for the boys too. They must be pretty gross jerks to want to touch the bitches. Good thing for them they lack the common decency to be humiliated by the way the boys treated and spoke about them.

Studying and getting good grades was something Elena enjoyed. The bitches also enjoyed good grades and that's why they made Elena do their homework. This is one of the rare times the bitches were almost nice to Elena. They needed something. Elena didn't mind doing their homework because it gave her leverage. They needed to "shut up" so she could finish even though it took mere minutes to complete it was a way for Elena to savor the silence.

Even when they entered high school the two were inseparable and asinine. They're hold over the boys seemed to wane. Boys were less interested in trashy girls and were more and more interested in the pretty cheerleaders, the girls who were nice. The two needed to go after the younger, less knowledgeable boys in the hopes of holding on to a sliver of popularity – as they called it. They squeaked into the 10th grade, failing tests but excelling on their homework.

High School. Yay! Almost done. Elena entered the 9th grade. Enough boys got the word that Jean and Tonya must have been adopted - first their fat and unattractive, second, they're really slutty and third they're morons. Nothing like the beautiful young lady Elena. School was great, friends were plentiful, and honor roll was easily obtained.

Not being a whore doesn't mean Elena doesn't like boys. One boy in particular…Vince was charming, handsome, and nice. Handsome may be an exaggeration for a 15-year-old boy, but he was close.

Vince asked Elena for her phone number, she sheepishly gave it to him as her friends giggled and encouraged her to let him call. This was the first boy that showed an interest in Elena and approached her. Friends would tell Elena that boys liked her, including her friend Anna's brother. She was shy when it came to the boys and more or less ignored them, so she wasn't quick to recognize if there was an interest.

Excited about Vince possibly calling, Elena smiled all the way home only to find Jean on the phone talking to one of her many guys telling them how she could please him so fast that he won't know what hit him and can't wait to get his dick in her mouth she was so incredibly vulgar yet somehow believed she was being seductive. Tonya was next to her sharing the phone saying he can compare and say who is better and dared to elaborate her experience.

Jean and Tonya whored it up for several minutes before solidifying a date and time laughing while eagerly anticipating their conquest. Tonya proudly questioned "You don't still want to talk to Elena, do you Vince?"

Elena was crushed. They just won't stop. Their laughter was the most annoying cackle that drones on much longer than necessary. Elena could almost smell their rotten breath through their crooked smiles. Staring probably a bit longer that she should have,

Elena took in all their ugly. Their disgusting faces, their freckled, ugly faces, their mean, nasty faces. Before she could catch herself, Elena muttered "You're so mean because you're both so ugly…I get it now". They're mouths fell open and they stammered for a comeback. Too late. Elena left the room and headed outside.

Okay, so Vince is not what Elena was looking for in a boyfriend. No more boys. They're all the same and so easily manipulated by Jean and Tonya. One day this won't be the case, she was sure of it. But who would want to bother with any boy who entertained either of those pigs? Boys can get a reputation too – and if word gets out that you were one of the boys who took pleasure in bedding one of the pigs, that could be just as damaging as the pigs who invited you to their playground.

Vince couldn't wait to see Elena the next day. He ran up to her begging to let him explain, talking about he was tricked, he didn't know what to say they were so persistent, he was just shocked at their behavior. Elena said it was okay, but she wasn't going to be dating anyone and hoped they would still be friends. Vince was saddened by this, he really liked Elena but had no choice. If Elena didn't want to go out with him, he wouldn't convince her so being her friend was the next best thing.

She did know what he was saying was true, but boys and her sisters just wasn't worth the drama. Elena did keep a friendship with Vince and the two of them hung out with a group of other friends several times. Nothing ever romantic happened between the two, it was just nice to be friends.

The days were rolling by, and the weeks turned into months. It's a few years off but Elena had to plan. Making plans for her future made her happy. Knowing she would be away from Jean and Tonya, away from their nastiness gave her something to look forward to. Elena will be able to create a life she deserves. The two didn't push Elena around as much now that Elena was becoming less tolerant of their torment.

There were times when the two seemed to be afraid of Elena. Perhaps because they couldn't break her. So many years they've tried to break Elena with their made-up stories, bullying, rudeness, anger, nothing worked.

Elena decided she would take a few classes at the vocational school. Cooking basics and baking. Thanks to her grandmother and dad teaching her some of their favorite recipes these classes came easy to her. The instructor felt Elena was much more advanced and didn't seem to need the guidance the other students required. Soufflés, risotto, paella, salmon, the cooking became more complex, and Elena exceled.

The bonus was bringing home treats for Artie and Helen. Artie would ask what he could pick up from the store so Elena could make dinners for them. Weekend trips to the market became a regular adventure – looking for new and exciting foods to prepare. Helen enjoyed not having to cook and trying new meals. The two skanks weren't too happy – never admitting how delicious the food was as they all but licked their plates clean. They also didn't like the new rule that since Elena cooked, they had to wash dishes. Another small victory for Elena.

Matteo was living on his own now and had a girlfriend, Anita. Artie was impressed that she was a schoolteacher, which he says is one of the most difficult jobs in the world. Anita was 5' 2" her blonde hair framed her slightly chubby face, her pale skin was flawless, her big brown eyes were so kind, she almost looked like a Disney princess.

Elena liked her immediately. Jean and Tonya pretended to. Anita talked a lot. It was fun to hear her talk about growing up in Chicago, her parents, and her younger sister. It was nice that she was close to her sister and a pleasure to hear that not all siblings are assholes. Stories about how she met Matteo, and their dates made him blush and Artie laugh. Anita was charming and made Matteo so happy.

Matteo's visits were limited to Sunday dinners - made by Elena, of course. Elena and Anita became quick friends sharing recipes, clothes, laughs, Elena finally had a real sister. Anita would pick up Elena to go to the mall, get their nails done, just spending time together was a joy. Matteo became an electrician and was very successful. Mom, Dad, and Elena were so proud.

Whenever Matteo came over Jean and Tonya would put on that fake high-pitched "hiiiii Anita" try to sit by her, tell her stories about Matteo (mostly lies) act as though they were the sweetest young ladies. Anita didn't like them, she was cordial. She could see how they were even without Matteo telling her the multitude of stories of all the crap they've done. The two gave up trying to win Anita over and continued just being the jackasses they have perfected.

It was a November wedding for Matteo and Anita. Anita's parents and her younger sister still live in Chicago, they came in for the wedding. Anita's sister Kathy was the life of the party, telling joke for joke with Matteo, she had an easy laugh and a sweet disposition. Anita's parents were more reserved they stayed mostly with their family members. The dance floor was filled with Matteo's buddies, Anita's friends, and most of Artie's family members. Jean and Tonya even hit the dance floor but soon after Helen gently nudged them off. The two kept hiking up their dresses far more than necessary and sexualized every dance move to the point of being X-rated.

The food was buffet style with the usual...pasta, beef, chicken, green beans, potatoes, etc. It was pretty good actually. They had a champagne fountain that Jean and Tonya were glued to when not on the dance floor - perhaps they were infused with liquid courage that may be an explanation for their vulgar dance moves. Perhaps. Helen finally was able to get them loaded into the back of Artie's car and left them there until Artie was ready to leave.

When the wedding was over Artie and Elena helped Helen into the car which was vibrating from the bitches snoring in the back. Artie had Elena sit up front with him and Helen then they headed home. If it weren't cold outside Artie would have left them sleeping in the car instead, he shook them awake, helped them balance as they made their way into the house. Elena helped Helen get into the house took of her shoes, poured her parents a small glass of wine and headed to bed. She knew just how to help her parents relax.

They talked about the wedding, leaving out all the embarrassing parts, and raved about how wonderful it was and how much the guests enjoyed themselves. They were so pleased Matteo found a nice girl to marry.

Matteo was eager to start a family, just like his parents, he always pictured himself being a dad and Anita was just the kind of woman you could see being a mom. Anita jokingly insisted on waiting until after the honeymoon. A beautiful 2-week European honeymoon gifted to them by Artie and Helen. They traveled all over Europe and came back with mounds of photos that took weeks to go through. Anita took photos of the food they ate so she can share with Elena who bought several picture frames for Anita's favorite honeymoon photos.

A few months later Anita told Elena she's going to have to buy more frames. Elena asked how many more honeymoon photos Anita was going to frame? Matteo laughed as Anita said "No, this one is for your niece or nephew." YAY!! Baby on board. Elena was immediately filled with joy and eager to meet the new family member that she already loved.

This was the best news ever. Artie and Helen were excited to welcome their first grandchild. Helen quickly began crocheting too many baby blankets, booties, sweaters, everything baby. Anita went from being a full-time teacher to a fill-in/substitute teacher so she could be home when she has her baby.

Anita and Matteo welcomed their son Angelo, he was the spitting image of Matteo. Elena was the obvious choice for Godmother, another reason for the bitches to not like her. Elena was the regular babysitter as Anita insisted Matteo still needs to date her. Anita was so sweet, and a great mom. Angelo was such a sweet baby and just too easy to fall in love with. Two years later they welcomed Anthony. Matteo was so proud to have two sons, he was a great dad just like Artie. His growing family was picture-perfect, he had every reason to be proud. Anita worked one or two days a week and Artie rushed to volunteer to care for his grandsons which worked out perfectly there's no better babysitter than grandpa.

Matteo and Anita bought a home just up the street from his mom and dad, so their visits were more frequent. Artie was down to working just one full time job and was eyeing retirement, he loved to have his grandsons visit as much as possible. Taking them for walks in the orchard and wooded areas was his favorite thing to do. Anita wasn't an umbrella mom – didn't hover over the boys, she let them be boys, have fun, play and be their sweet selves. She loved Matteo's parents were so close to her sons since her family never left Chicago. They did visit a few times and sent gifts, it just wasn't feasible for them to come every week.

Tonya seemed to hate Matteo's sons, if not hate, she certainly had a strong dislike for them always pushing them away and ignoring them. Ignoring sweet babies, being mean, her typical behavior. She never verbally said anything to them just shot them looks that even an infant can recognize as nasty. Jean was just weird with them demanding respect and that they pronounce her name correctly. They're babies! Jean would loudly mouth "ANNNNTTT GEEEE EEENNN" Matteo would whisper to Elena "DUUUMB BIIIITTTCHHH" and they would laugh.

Elena was quick to scoop them up and cover them in too many kisses. Who can possibly be hateful to a small child? Elena talking to her friends would say "We grew up in the same house, how are they so different?" None of Elena's friends cared for her sisters, no one really liked them, there was not much to like. They were selfish, judgmental – as if they had a right to be, eager to hog the spotlight and get whatever attention they could. Elena was lucky that her friends met her before her sisters, or she may never have had the chance to make friends.

Artie witnessed Jean hand Angelo a toy – this was astounding. There were glimmers of decency every now and again. Glimmers. And not very often. Any hint of kindness from the two and Helen would revel and hold on to hope that maybe they were on the cusp of growing up and becoming less of an embarrassment. She was often embarrassed by her two daughters obvious by her uncomfortable need to fill silence or change a subject to avoid either of them opening their mouths in front of guests.

The high school years continued with the same ole same ole. Upon graduation, yes, they graduated! Jean landed a job at a local gas station where she stole cigarettes and let her boyfriend fill his car for free. She had a boyfriend for about a month giving him free gas and cigarettes was her way of keeping him interested. It didn't take long before the station owner learned she was giving away gasoline and stealing cigarettes and she was soon fired.

She told Artie that she quit because the owner couldn't afford to pay her. No one believed her. No one ever believed her it didn't take anyone too long after meeting her to understand she can't be trusted. Tonya worked at a fast-food restaurant and would brag that she's entitled to a free lunch. She missed the key wording "A" free lunch. Her mouth was always full of food, whether it be fries from someone's order, or a piece of chicken off a plate that fit perfectly into her fat mouth. The whole stealing thing was something she and Jean had in common. Tonya was always stuffing her purse with snacks to eat on the way home or to enjoy later in bed.

Tonya tried to get Jean a job at the restaurant, but Jean claimed she couldn't work. Jean wasn't going to share her secret just yet, but telling Tonya was just as bad as taking an ad out in the newspaper. Everyone found out immediately that Jean was pregnant. Twenty years old and pregnant with no job. Jean claiming her pregnancy was special and different from most said she was told not to work. Again, liar. No one told her that. Word probably got out about her being a thief.

She didn't get the same response as when Anita announced her pregnancy. She didn't expect any degree of excitement from Artie which was good, she wasn't disappointed in his non-reaction. She moved into a makeshift bedroom in the basement. The walls were finished and there was a nice, carpeted area. She claimed to need privacy in her 'condition'. Tonya and Elena now had their own rooms. They had to share once Matteo moved out and Jean took over his room but for whatever reason she felt more comfortable in the basement now that she was "with child".

Tonya wasn't happy she never got a "big" bed. The bunk beds were taken apart and one given to Elena the other to Tonya, who argued she needed a bigger bed not one for a child. The beds were fine. Tonya was just too big. Tonya's room was always unkempt with dirty clothes covering the floors she did the sniff-test to see if something would pass for clean when she would go out. Elena's treasured rock from Champ and stuffed toy from David - that was hand washed because it had been in the fort for so long - were now displayed on her dresser. Artie put a lock on Elena's bedroom door knowing it was to keep the bitches out, Elena was very grateful for his kindness. Tonya begged for a lock too but that never happened Helen told her she needed to get in the room to gather up the dirty laundry and clean the room. Tonya was good with that explanation, having Helen do her laundry and clean her room was worth going without a lock.

Jean was smart to stay in the basement area to avoid Artie. His displeasure with the situation was oftentimes hard to restrain. Helen wasn't happy either, but it was too late to do anything, and she wanted to make the best of the situation. Jean would call up to Helen to bring her food or snacks and Helen obediently obliged as if she were a hired maid. Tonya took the pregnancy as a chance to voice to everyone how great *her* life is and she's smart enough to not get pregnant. Poking those when they're down. She's relentless.

Tonya taunting Jean saying she's so fat now they'll have to grease the doorway so she could get out of the house. This of course would make Jean cry and exclaim "Think about the baby! The baby! Stop!" Tonya always the button pusher. Even when they were getting along Tonya on occasion would refer to Jean as "Big Nose" which unbelievably threw Jean into a fit of convulsing tears as if "Big Nose" was the most crushing insult ever. The two had an odd relationship spewing insults and anger at each other one moment and laughing together at someone else's expense the next.

Helen bringing down Jean's many snacks was informed that it was imperative that a baby shower be thrown and was handed a list of foods to prepare and relatives to invite. Her baby was special, and everyone needed to spoil Jean because she was alone and claimed to be suffering a difficult pregnancy and the reason for her excessive weight gain. Her pregnancy was not difficult, just a story she came up with to gain sympathy and attention.

Helen threw the baby shower and invited all the relatives as instructed. Certain they only came out of respect for Artie and Helen. Jean was brazen enough to send out her list of gifts she wanted including a $400 rocking chair, $800 crib, and ridiculously expensive items that she had nowhere to store. The baby shower was uneventful, and the relatives were incredibly generous. Artie's sisters bought the rocking chair and other gifts, Artie and Helen bought the crib and stroller. Everything she could need for the baby was provided including several boxes of diapers.

Helen's nephew's wife came to the shower and there was some chatter going around. Tonya had someone to gossip about again - her favorite pastime. Martha was perhaps the "senior" version of Tonya and Jean. A well-known tramp. The stories of her escapades outside the confines of her marriage including her husband's brother were well-known to all the family. Most of them just didn't care because her husband was a jerk always something shady going on with that guy. Martha was vulgar, always cussed, a cigarette hanging from her unevenly applied lipstick mouth, she didn't believe in bras or decent skirt lengths, decency of any kind was not her forte.

As the shower came to an end, Tonya quizzically asked about why the daddy's family didn't show. Of course, she knew, always the troublemaker stirring the pot starting the rumors savoring the uncomfortable atmosphere she's created. Helen was quick to change the subject and the relatives were polite enough to act as though they didn't hear Tonya's comments.

Truth is Jean didn't know who the father was and probably didn't care. Another reason for Artie to be disappointed in the way she behaved. Jean was a smoker and being pregnant didn't stop her nicotine addiction which may have led to the baby being born a month early. When the baby was born, she said she knew the father was one of two men because the beautiful baby girl was black, and she only remembers sleeping with two black men. The baby had a headful of beautiful curls, large eyes, and perfect lips. Must look like the father.

She was lucky that one of the men stepped up and accepted responsibility. From what little interaction the family had with Conrad, he seemed like a very nice man, he worked as a trash collector for the city. Jean and Conrad moved into a trailer together they seemed happy. Artie gave them a sizeable about of money to get their life in order hoping it would help his grandbaby. It was a good thing that Conrad had a job and Jean had someone to help take care of her – that was one responsibility Artie did not want to deal with.

No one knew what they used the money for, they just assumed it was to purchase a better trailer. Artie wanted to make certain his grandbaby was cared for; he adored the little baby. Helen crocheted several blankets and bought far too many darling outfits for her new granddaughter. Jean expected it and didn't seem too appreciative. The family was able to see the baby for a few months while Jean and Conrad readied the new trailer for the baby's arrival.

The baby was about 4 months old when Jean stopped coming around. She got all the money she would be getting from Artie, Helen wasn't buying any more clothes, so there was no reason. They didn't need anything, so why bother coming over. Helen missed her new granddaughter, but Jean chose not to speak to her mom and dad because she could no longer fool them and was called out on too many of her lies.

The lying on her part was so unnecessary yet constant. Just lied to lie about anything and everything. Helen believed her two daughters needed to be medicated, never told them that because their reactions would have been a nightmare to deal with, but medication couldn't hurt.

Tonya called Jean every now and again, but that was just to make Tonya feel better about herself. Tonya wanted to make sure that Jean was still miserable, wasn't working, her man was cheating on her, everything that made Tonya happy and how she enjoyed sharing the misfortunes with anyone who would listen. You know this by now, it's her favorite pastime to revel in the misery of others.

If Jean could land a man, then Tonya felt she could too. It was her mission to do better than Jean and make sure everyone knew she was better. It would be interesting to see just what kind of man Tonya would be able to attract. There's someone for everyone, right?

Tonya started taking diet pills and stool softeners to lose weight. She was able to get down to a size 14, and actually looked presentable. She became a bank teller and landed a boyfriend. Wouldn't say this made her better than Jean, she would. But no one else would. Elena was happy for her, maybe the happier Tonya became, the nicer she would be. Eh. It's a stretch.

Tonya smiled every now and again, showered more than twice a week and started to clean up her room. Announcing now that she's a skinny size 14 she's going to need new clothes and Helen should probably help buy her some clothes. This conversation happened when Artie was at work of course. And of course, Helen took her shopping and spent more money than she should have.

Could a boyfriend have this much influence over a monster? Apparently. Tonya worked on herself attempting to play nice when around the family and complained a hell of a lot less. Too bad she didn't find a boyfriend when she was 2!

Tonya's boyfriend, Billy moved to the neighborhood from Kentucky. He was easy going, a few years older than Tonya, quick to offer a loud guttural laugh and show his toothy grin. His light brown hair fell just to his shoulders, a slight hint of balding. Billy was a lanky 6' 3" towering over Tonya's 5' 1" frame. Yet they fit well together. She was eager to show him off to the family. She got a man. It was finally her time to shine and show how much better she was than Jean.

Matteo had a cookout and Tonya accepted the invitation to bring along her boyfriend. She never came to family cookouts or get-togethers; she didn't like to be around her family. Everyone hoped this was a turning point and that she would become a better person, a kinder person, one that Helen wouldn't be ashamed to claim as her own. Billy was quick to introduce himself to everyone with a too tight handshake and a quick grin. He tried giving Helen a hug which was interrupted by Matteo handing him a beer much to the gratitude of Helen.

Angelo and Anthony were playing kick ball in the back of the house, Billy gleefully shouted "Aw man, I love kids. I can't wait to have a houseful!" Tonya said "Oh me too" as she reached over to pick up a startled Anthony who fussed his way out of her clutches. Matteo and Elena were mesmerized by her behavior, flipping her hair, laughing, being pleasant something they've never witnessed such human-like qualities from Tonya. Anita talking with Elena said, "Could you imagine her as a mother?" Oh hell no. No. Those poor children.

She really put on a show for Billy going on and on about how much she loves children and would babysit whenever she could. She never babysat; she hated kids. Billy examined Matteo's home as if he was an inspector looking for trouble spots and asked whose house was in the back. It was actually a barn; Matteo took Billy back to check it out.

Matteo had just over 15 acres of property and just had the two-story barn built which was so nice his friend wanted to live in it. Billy said he would too, it was pretty fancy with a poured concrete floor and finished walls and ceilings. The four stalls were spacious with huge windows and ceiling fans with one main door leading to the fenced in pasture.

Billy asked what kind of animals he would be getting, Matteo told him he planned on getting some goats, chickens and maybe a cow too. Billy helped himself to another beer as they headed back to the house while they continued talking about the barn and their fondness for animals and pets. Matteo of course thought about Champ but didn't say anything, it was too painful to talk about and the questionable way he passed away was not something Matteo wanted to relive.

Billy said he always liked animals and had two cats. He found them when they were kittens naming them cat and kitty which were now 7 years old. Insisting his cats play fetch and guard the house better than any dog he ever knew. More than likely an exaggeration yet he was so convincingly animated as he talked about his cats which he likened to cougars maybe he was telling the truth.

Billy had fun stories about growing up in Kentucky, told his fishing and hunting tales and shared his squirrel recipes exclaiming everyone was missing out "squirrel is deeelishious." Matteo asked how many squirrels Billy had to eat to be full, Billy quickly answered 5 and everyone laughed. Even Billy laughed, he didn't care. He was likeable and harmless. Good Ole boy just looking for his next beer and a good woman.

Tonya spent a lot of time at Billy's house – another reason to like Billy, he kept her away from the family. When she did come home, she was not that unpleasant. Billy was good for her and perhaps she was on her way to becoming a tolerable human being. The only sticking point for Tonya was her dislike for Billy's cats. The cats must have sensed her dislike as they avoided being near her yet readily greeted and snuggled with Billy who was oblivious to Tonya's dislike of his cherished kitties.

One day Tonya told Elena she needed her to pick up Billy's two cats because they had an appointment to be "put down" claiming they were on death's door and she couldn't do it, she and Billy were going camping for the weekend and she wanted those cats gone before she got back. She had no one else to ask and assured Billy it would be taken care of because Billy's heart is breaking, and he shouldn't be forced to 'do the right thing'. You can't just put down cats because you don't like them!

There was nothing wrong with these beautiful cats she convinced Billy they were sick and urinating all over the house. Convincingly explaining to him several veterinarians told her there was nothing to do and they all recommended they be put down because that's what is best for the cats, so they don't suffer any longer. Billy was devastated but since that was what the veterinarians said he should do, he agreed to let her take care of the details as it pained him too much to lose his two little sweeties. Tonya just didn't like them. She is just so evil.

Elena was pleased that she was tasked with this disgusting request and assured Tonya, she would pick them up and she would never see them again. Tonya enjoyed the fact that Elena was going to take the cats knowing that she was such an animal lover this would definitely cause Elena great pain. Matteo knew Elena wasn't going to have the cats euthanized and said those cats were lucky that Tonya was too stupid to realize that.

Elena went to Billy's house and picked up the cats. A calico and a striped tiger cat – the sweetest kitties. Tonya left $50 in an envelope with strict instructions to dump them at the vet to be killed. Elena, of course did NOT euthanize the cats. Instead, she took them to a no-kill shelter and donated the $50 for their care. Elena stopped by the next day and donated several bags of food, treats and litter along with a monetary donation to which Artie and Matteo added a large sum.

When Billy and Tonya returned from their camping trip, Tonya stopped by Artie and Helen's and was telling them how distraught she was about the cats, and she couldn't stop crying all weekend. Had she been paying attention to anyone but herself she may have noticed Artie's exaggerated eye roll and snicker as he knew exactly what happened to the cats. She went on to say how Billy's friends, even Billy, were comforting her and just how sad it was. Really? If she ever found out that they were living happily together at a nice home, she would be livid.

It took just 4 days for the two cats to get adopted. The best part was they were adopted together. Tonya never found out that they were not euthanized, and she took such pleasure in 'meowing' when she walked past Elena. What happened to her being nice? Gotta take it when you can. It's sporadic yet there are occasions where she's almost human.

Billy would not be getting any more pets. Tonya convinced him they were too much work and since they both enjoyed camping (yes, she hated camping), they wouldn't have to find anyone to care for pets when they were gone. She had a way of convincing

Billy everything she said was right, that his best interest was always the basis of her decisions.

Tonya continued her work as a bank teller no one was sure what Billy did for work, it was always "construction" or "helping out a friend". They've been dating for several months now and Tonya was already talking marriage. Everyone felt as though she knew Billy was more than likely her only option. Billy was easy going, just going with the flow kind of guy that was thrilled to have a woman that had a job and that he could land a too-wet kiss on whenever he pleased.

Tonya still made the occasional call to Jean to brag about how well she was doing and to bait stories about how things weren't so good for Jean. Feigning sympathy for Jean's misfortunes when Billy was in earshot made him believe that she gave a damn about anyone but herself. She would share the stories about Jean with Billy with tears in her eyes stressing how much she cared. Billy liked everyone and wanted everyone to have a good time and be happy. He liked things simple.

Elena graduated high school and Tonya offered to take her out to "celebrate" before she heads off to college. Elena, always the optimist, believed Tonya was trying to make amends, dare I say even be nice perhaps it's one of those rare moments. Hanging out with Tonya would make Helen happy so that was another reason for Elena to accept. Tonya said they would be going to a cookout at Billy's friend's house so don't dress up. Elena threw on a pair of jeans and tee-shirt paired with her favorite beat up sneakers - perfect for a "Billy" event. Elena planned to be extra careful not to be fooled into eating squirrel.

Billy pulled up in a brown 1980 Chevy Nova, two doors and less rust than expected. Billy hopped out and moved the seat for Elena to get into the back. Dammit. Company. There was a man in the back grinning with excitement as if this were a date. Seems Billy and Tonya were expecting just that.

Roger was eager for Elena to join him in the back seat and couldn't wait to introduce himself. Roger was stupid grinning showing a gap where a tooth once was under his untamed moustache, his baseball cap backward – must be a rebel - his curly hair so tight that if he could, Elena would bet he'd have a mullet. He was a mechanic; you'd know this without him telling you by the dirt under his fingernails. His breath reeked of cheap beer. Shit. How the hell can Elena escape this fool? Reminder: Never get in a backseat if the car doesn't have four doors. Always have a backup plan should things not go as planned.

Tonya kept looking back at Elena knowing she was incredibly uncomfortable with this deliverance hillbilly wanna be. Tonya would smirk and laugh. She knew just what she was doing. Elena worried about the endgame. What was this bitch's master plan?! Elena was angry at herself for accepting the invitation and even for a moment was angry with Helen. She really couldn't blame the fact that hanging out with Tonya pleased Helen, but this was just so messed up. Breathe. Just Breathe. It'll be over soon. Hopefully. She wasn't angry at Helen she just couldn't believe she was so damn stupid to think Tonya could have been anything but a fucking bitch.

Roger sucking down a beer, brought out a bottle of whisky. Slugged right out of the bottle, then very gentleman-like offered it up to Elena for a swig. She politely declined. Tonya explained "Oh she's a prude, we'll loosen her up soon enough" they all laughed. Okay, this is not a celebration. This is not okay. This is a problem.

When Billy cracked open a beer that's when Elena couldn't hold her tongue any longer. "Put the fucking beer down Billy!" Tonya told her to mind her own business. They argued as Elena said "This IS my business, I'm in the car you assholes!" Wow being argumentative with Tonya in front of her man was more than Tonya could bear, she attempted to leap over the seat to assault Elena, but her fat ass couldn't make it. The guys just laughed as Billy told Tonya she's too chunky to be hoping over car seats he handed her a beer and told her to settle her ass down. Tonya was getting bigger now that she landed her man. Billy claimed didn't mind he would joke "more to love" and it was better than her weekly clogging of the toilet with her overuse of laxatives.

After about 20 minutes in the backseat squeezed as far as she possibly could from stink breath Roger, Elena became concerned when Billy went off the road and turned down a dirt path, not a road, just a path into some woods. At first she believed he was drunk and didn't know where he was going, he was driving into acres and acres of woods, his car bounced between ditches, a hub-cap popped off and rolled an impressive distance before landing in some weeds, branches scraped the car doors and windows. Billy had his window down and a branch hit his arm and caught the bottom of his chin leaving a small scratch. Roger was yelling incoherently perhaps attempting to sing, you really couldn't tell. Oh damn. That "deliverance hillbilly" thought was more on the mark than expected. All Elena could do at this point was to pray. She held on tight and prayed quietly that they would be safe, and she would get home without being harmed.

Finally coming to a huge opening in the woods there were about 5 other cars parked in random areas. "We're here" Billy exclaimed as he almost forgot to put the car in park. Jumping from the car Billy quickly pushed the seat forward for Elena to get out. Tonya and Roger were already out on the passenger side of the car. Billy opened the trunk of the car and removed a large Styrofoam cooler – nothing but the best for asshat and his toothless pal – it was filled with cans of beer floating in cold water his driving caused most of the water to slosh out into the trunk. The water was probably ice at one point.

The freedom of getting out of that car is so underrated. Away from stink breath and Tonya's devious, ugly face. Stepping out of the car Elena quickly glanced around. There were several couples, maybe 20 people, all enjoying adult beverages and a roaring bonfire. No food. She hastened to get away from Tonya and headed over to a less threatening looking group.

Roger came up next to Elena and attempted to put an arm around her, she quickly stepped out of that mess and walked up to two women. Elena was quick to start a conversation looking for an escape from the three losers that brought her there. Tammy and Leslie were actually pretty nice, not the kind of folks that Elena would normally seek out as friends, with their tattoos, beer swilling, loud mouths, but they were at this moment the lesser of two evils. Talking with the two women it was necessary to dumb-down the conversation and just stick to cars and marijuana. Nothing Elena knew anything about, so she quietly walked away creating a distance between herself and the bulk of the crowd.

Elena wanted out, but she knew she would not get back into Billy's car. The group of partiers were loud, not sure any of them bathed in the last week, a few of them had all their teeth. This was a hodgepodge of hillbilly, losers, and homeless. Game plan. How to escape these losers…too far to walk, or is it?

Maybe Elena could sneak down the dirt path find the road and then what? This was not ideal. Searching the crowd to determine the least disgusting person and if anyone there would be kind enough to take her home was fruitless. They were cookie cutter. Their behaviors mimicked one another they laughed too loud, drank too much, and hooped and hollered at nothing. At one point Roger ducked behind a car to barf up some of that whisky he chugged on the drive over. Pouring whisky in his mouth to rinse the remnants of vomit he was ready to get back to the party.

Music can be a wonderful enhancement to any event but when it's blasted at a level that shakes the ground there's a clue it's far too loud. If you didn't know they were actually dancing, you might call an ambulance thinking they were having seizures or maybe believe you walked into a strip club where they tip dancers with loose change. The women were pulling up their tank tops showing off their tatted boobs while the men encouraged them to take off more.

It was a relief more than the crowd knew that Tonya decided to keep on her shirt. Billy came up behind her grabbing her breasts with both hands saying "These are mine" she giggled as if it was a form of flattery.

The beers and drinks were flowing, and the fire roared. Elena was handed a beer, she took the beer without thanking whoever the man was - she didn't know anyone but the two ladies she briefly spoke with, Tonya, Billy and now Roger. Trying to make the best of a bad situation wasn't going to happen, there was nothing good about this and there was no hope that it would get better.

After about an hour of not drinking the beer that was handed her Elena decided to go for a walk. Just as she started to get a reasonable distance between herself and the drunks, Tonya began yelling "Bitch get over here and quit being so fucking stuck up, you think you're too good for us? You Bitch!" That riled up the rest of the hillbillies who started yelling in agreement with Tonya calling Elena a slew of names and moving toward her.

Elena felt her face flush with panic as Roger quickly made his way within feet of her, shoving a bottle of discolored booze at her demanding she take a swig. "Drink you fucking bitch, you too good for us?!" Elena slapped the bottle from his filthy hand then kicked his knee in causing him to fall to the ground. She was quickly surrounded by the gang of losers and was shoved to the ground by one of the women she had spoken with earlier, she quickly jumped to her feet impressing the drunks who were stammering and struggling to come up with clever insults. Desperately assessing the situation her eyes rapidly searching for a way out then it happened. The most beautiful flash of red and blue lights quickly closing in from a distance. Undoubtedly Elena was the only one who was pleased to see the police lights.

The hillbillies jumped into their cars they were so quick and anxious to get out the fools even left most of their beer behind. Their tires kicked up a ton of dirt and debris that sprayed into the fire causing a lot of smoke to cover the area which made it easy for several of them to escape. "HURRY UP" Tonya yelled to Elena. Nope. Elena stayed right there. Cops were so much better than the backseat with stink breath and a drunk driver behind the wheel. "Leave the Bitch! Let's go!" Ordered Tonya.

There were 3 police cars coming down the path Elena waited by a tree until things settled down. Two police cars followed the cars that were fleeing. The third car stopped behind Billy's car. HA! This made Elena so happy. The jerks were getting busted. So was she. She was there too. The officer jumped from his car with his K-9. What a beautiful dog - knew just who to go after and took

Billy down effortlessly Billy's screams of pain as the dog chomped on his ass were the best music of the night, while the K-9 was doing his job the officer barely gave chase before he caught and cuffed Roger who was so unstable, he couldn't even sit. Tonya was crying. So predictable. Let's see how Elena gets blamed for this mess.

After securing the two jerks the officer approached Tonya who unfortunately urinated all over herself. Tonya wailed as she hugged her handcuffed boyfriend. He told her to get off him because she was wet and stunk and he didn't want piss all over him. This made her wail even louder, in response Billy offered quick reassurance that she's pretty and she's his woman, he just don't want no pee on him that's all. This tactic didn't work so Roger yelled at her to stop the drama before they get into more trouble. It was actually funny to watch the losers demise. The only thing missing was a comfortable chair and popcorn.

It was obvious the officer was angry at the mess he poured the water from the Styrofoam cooler on the fire then kicked dirt on it to make sure it was completely out. Not even noticing there was another person there the officer dusted off his slacks, pet his dog who was looking past him almost smiling at Elena. She had no fear of the dog and walked up to the officer, attempting to explain she thought she was being taken to a cookout, hadn't had anything to drink and had no way home.

The officer was distracted by the three he had already dealt with, getting his K-9 back into the vehicle and calling on his radio for assistance in getting the guys to the jail that he barely noticed Elena. Annoyed he quickly looked up. Then he slowly looked up. Then he just looked. Damn this girl is beautiful. Then he noticed she was petting Zeus, his K-9 through the open car window. No one pets Zeus, he's a dangerous dog. No one but Elena. He was impressed that Zeus connected to this woman so quickly and allowed her to touch him, dogs know. If Zeus says she's a good person, she's a good person.

Okay. This evening just went from bad to worse to damn good. This was one of the best-looking men Elena had ever seen.

Big muscular arms covered in tattoos; Elena heard of "chiseled" features before but now she understood. WOW. Strong face, clean shaven, broad shoulders, his hair cut in a gentleman's cut, his eyes are the darkest most beautiful eyes with lashes that only girls should have. Oh and that smile. Perfect teeth. Beautiful.

Officer Dominic asked Elena what she was doing there. Again, she explained in detail the unfortunate trust in her sister for planning a celebratory evening. Helping to validate her story, Roger yelled "Bitch you fucking nark, you didn't drink so you could rat us out, you bitch" his drunken ramblings continued until another officer arrived and put him and Billy in the back of his car.

Dominic was familiar with the usual clientele, using that term loosely, that frequented the party woods as they referred to the area, he'd never seen Elena before he was sure this wasn't her usual crowd and believed Zeus confirmed that. Elena didn't get any citations or in any trouble at all, not just because she was so pretty, but the officer knew she was just in the wrong place at the wrong time and trusted the wrong people.

Getting a ride home in a police car was a pleasure for Elena as she and Dominic talked for the 30 plus minute ride, that same ride was horrifying for Tonya who sat on a huge plastic tarp to avoid getting urine all over the car in the back with Zeus! There was a divider, one side for the K-9 and the other for distraught Tonya clutching her citations and insisting she didn't pee herself it was water- explain this one to mommy.

When the police car pulled into the driveway, Artie was just arriving home from work. Again, this evening is getting better and better. Officer Dominic and Elena exited the vehicle. Artie ran up not knowing what to expect, then the officer opened the rear door to let Tonya out. Artie could see had wet herself and she was visibly drunk, he was mortified. Police officers don't come to Artie's home. This is so embarrassing; the neighbors will talk. Tonya made her way into the house quickly to get away from Artie.

Officer Dominic introduced himself to Artie and explained what had happened and that Elena was not getting cited because she hadn't had anything to drink and was taken there under false pretense. Artie was put at ease but still so embarrassed by the trouble Tonya had caused. He knew Elena was a good girl and although he could never prove it, he knew Jean and Tonya were the ones causing all the problems and troubles. Couldn't prove it until now.

Elena said goodbye to Dominic and thanked him for the ride. Dominic was happy to meet Elena's father but hoped to have more time to muster up the courage to ask for her phone number. Artie smiled as Elena went into the house. Helen was furious at Elena for not stopping Tonya from drinking. What? Okay. Here we go again…

When Artie came in the house Helen began to complain that she couldn't believe Elena would let this happen to Tonya. Artie stopped her before she could finish. Enough. He knew Helen felt sorry for Tonya for being heavier, nowhere near as pretty as Elena. But he wasn't going to allow this to go on any longer. Tonya hid in her bedroom for the next few days and avoided seeing Artie for fear of being punished.

Artie told the neighbors that the police officer was a good friend of the family and since Billy's car broke down, he was nice enough to give his daughters a ride home. Artie wasn't someone to tell lies, but he wanted to protect his integrity and reputation. It was a harmless enough fib.

Billy and Roger were lucky enough to spend the night in jail on the comfortable cots and enjoy a free breakfast courtesy of the taxpayers. After a few days Billy felt it would be okay if he came over and apologized to Artie and said he was just meeting up with friends and didn't realize they'd be drinking and partying the way they were.

Artie knew better, but he also knew Tonya probably couldn't do any better than Billy. Tonya was off the hook. Even better, they decided to move in together. Billy's friend had a two-bedroom house for rent about a 45 minute ride from Artie and Helen's home. The relief on Helen's face that Tonya was leaving the house and moving in with a man was uncontainable. In her book this was a success for Tonya and a load off Helen's shoulders.

As Tonya packed up her belongings, she helped herself to some of Helen's jewelry, and some of Artie's collectibles When Artie noticed his belongings were missing, Helen made excuses. Helen never mentioned anything about her missing jewelry. It was just stuff that Tonya was certain to pawn for a few bucks.

It was the following Saturday the phone rang and was quickly answered mid-ring. Artie was obviously thrilled with the seemingly expected call, chatting as though it was an old friend. "Elena, phone call" Artie announced. Puzzled, Elena took the phone. Dominic. She felt her face flush. Dominic explained when Elena went into the house last week, he spoke with her dad and asked if he could take her out. Dominic wouldn't be off work until Tuesday, so he asked if Elena would like to go to dinner. She may have said yes before he completed the question.

Tuesday couldn't come fast enough. Now that Tuesday was here, Elena was sure she wouldn't have enough time to get ready. The pile of dresses that didn't make the cut were strewn across the bed and floor. Finally, the perfect, well, suitable, not quite perfection, dress was selected. It was lovely. Elena was just stressing over her date. The dress was sky blue, very delicate, peppered with light yellow flowers - almost an afterthought in the creation. The dress fell just below the knee so a high heel may have been overkill for this simple dress so the look was finished off with a lovely yellow kitten heel. Her long hair down in loose curls and very minimal makeup. She was perfect.

Artie greeted Dominic at the door and brought him in to meet Helen. Her eyes widened when she looked up and saw this handsome man. He was wearing a light blue polo shirt and jeans with boat shoes. To see Elena and Dominic together they looked like they came from a magazine with their flattering outfits - it was kismet.

Best. Date. Ever. Elena never knew the feeling of being the focus of someone's full attention. Dominic was complimentary, gentlemanly, and so handsome. Dominic loved Elena's beautiful smile, sparkling eyes, kind nature and great sense of humor. They talked about family and growing up, Dominic was an only child and his mom passed away when he was young. They talked about their dreams and hopes for their futures and what they most looked forward to.

As Dominic pulled into the driveway to drop Elena off, neither of them wanted the date to end. It was late, and it was time to say goodbye. Dominic walked over and opened Elena's car door, as she stepped out, he put his strong, tattooed arm on the car to block her in the open door. As Elena stood there anticipating his lips on hers, he kissed her. The kiss was gentle, passionate, kind, and honest. The feeling you have when you kiss someone that you connect with is bewitching. They both felt the intense warmth, the pureness of their affection, hearts beating faster, not wanting to leave one another. This moment is one that should last an eternity.

Text messages and phone calls were constant and long. Dominic and Elena saw one another at every possible opportunity. The depth of their affection grew with each touch, it was in every conversation, solidified by their mutual respect and kind hearts. Artie was so pleased that Elena was dating Dominic. He liked that Dominic had a great job, was gentlemanly, respectful and that Elena adored him and he her.

Elena was going to college; it was only 45 minutes from home and this way she can still see Dominic regularly. Their routines didn't change much since Elena was still living at home.

Elena decided to study business management/hospitality. Elena wanted to work in a restaurant but wanted to know how to run a restaurant from top to bottom. Elena soon added culinary school to her already packed schedule and eventually became an employee of the culinary school. The pay was great, and she continued to learn while working.

There was always time for Dominic. Elena would come home and make dinner for Artie and Helen, oftentimes Dominic joined them for dinner it felt so natural to have him sharing a meal with Elena and her parents. They were always excited to see what Elena was going to create, it was almost unnecessary to wash the dishes as everyone seemed to lick their plates clean.

Artie told Elena she should open her own restaurant. He always said this, has been since she was 12. Elena wasn't ready for that, she wanted to continue working at the culinary school and be fully prepared to be successful. Owning a restaurant. That seemed like a far-fetched dream for Elena.

Everything seemed to be falling into place. Matteo and Anita had a great family of their own, lovely home, great jobs, Elena and Dominic were inseparable, he had a great job, Elena was working toward her dream of working in a restaurant, Artie and Helen were enjoying their time together going to play bingo, the casinos, having friends over or just going out to dinner. They were happy.

Speaking of happy…

Billy and Tonya got married. They went to their city hall and were married by a judge. The family found out when Tonya sent out notices of her wedding registry asking for gifts. Artie and Helen sent her a huge check with their congratulations. Matteo left it up to Anita to buy whatever she felt was necessary, Elena bought several of their items off their registry, Dominic even bought a few items for them. The absolute best part of Tonya getting married to Billy is his last name is LARGE. TON-YA LARGE. Matteo's jokes were endless.

Helen called Tonya and told her she'd like to have a small party to celebrate her wedding. Of course, Tonya loved this idea as she was going to be the center of attention. Tonya let Helen know what foods she wanted served, gave the names of 27 of Billy's friends/family members that would be coming and then requested a DJ. Okay, this small party just got big and expensive. It was as if she was expecting the phone call and offer of a party. She was fully prepared with her lists.

Helen tasked Elena with cooking for the wedding, she never cooked for such a big crowd, but was excited for the challenge. Tonya requested burgers, corn, mashed potatoes, hot dogs, baked beans and a huge chocolate wedding cake - the list was ridiculous. Artie told Elena there was reason for her to help with anything he knew how badly Tonya treated her. Elena said she didn't mind because it was less stress for Helen and good practice for her to cook for a large group of people. She was always quick to forgive and even quicker to lend a helping hand.

Elena called Matteo who had a spit to roast meat and asked him if he could roast a side of beef - something Matteo has done on several occasions and always delicious. Matteo was happy to help. Elena included small corn on the cob, green beans, mashed potatoes, ugh hot dogs? Okay this is what Tonya wants so hot dogs and baked beans. Elena added several fancy hors d'oeuvres, charcuterie boards and fruit platters to make the celebration seem less "cheap".

The August wedding celebration was worrisome, but luckily wasn't as hot as the previous days reaching a high of 76. Two large white tents in Artie and Helen's backyard housed the linen draped tables with a smaller tent housing the tables loaded with the delicious foods Elena created. Fans offered a nice breeze to keep the 50+ guests comfortable. Elena made a stunning wedding cake sprinkled with fresh edible flowers and adorned with the customary bride and groom topper.

There was no DJ, just a stereo system with several tasteful CDs so the music would continue throughout the celebration. This was much too pretty a wedding for Tonya, it made Helen happy that it did look so lovely she wouldn't be too uncomfortable when the family met Billy.

Tonya and Billy arrived after most of the guests. Tonya wearing a short white dress that was too snug and her now large boobs (the ones she always wanted in high school) were spilling out of her dress. Matteo joked to Elena how strong the seams must be. Billy wore black slacks that drooped and nearly fell off whenever he bent over to kiss an aunt or greet a friend, a white shirt that was at times tucked into his pants and a green tie.

Matteo tended to the 35-pound beef on the spit as Billy and his friends reached in to try and snatch a slice off as it turned. Everyone, including Tonya, loved the food - even the hot dogs!

Elena was happy to have done this for Tonya and Billy and was pleased they were happy. It was a test to see if Elena could pull off feeding a large crowd of people, she was pleased with the outcome. Dominic came after his shift so most of the guests had already eaten. Elena saved him a fresh plate of food and enjoyed dinner with him. Dominic was always so grateful for everything Elena did for him, it wasn't forced she showed kindness and thoughtfulness to everyone. Watching Elena with her nephews, smiling with her family, laughing with Matteo, everything about her was captivating.

Dominic and Elena were in the house enjoying one another's company when one of the wedding guests stumbled into the kitchen. The guest looked up and said "Oh shit" after recognizing Dominic as the police officer that arrested him months ago. Roger hurried by as Elena and Dominic shared a laugh at Roger's expense. Dominic teased he was going to put his uniform back on and sit by Roger. After finishing up their delicious dinner Dominic and Elena headed out to the celebration.

Dominic and Matteo have met several times, he joined Elena in babysitting Matteo's boys. They all loved Dominic. Matteo took Dominic aside and offered him a cigar. Neither of them smoked, Matteo enjoyed an occasional cigar Dominic opted for a glass of wine instead. The two men could be heard laughing from 30 feet away. No doubt Matteo was telling a slew of jokes or making jokes about the lovely newlyweds.

Anita and Elena were starting to clean up after the guests as the party was winding down. The trash bags were quickly filling with discarded cups, plates, and napkins. Anita and Elena threw the trash bags into the back of Matteo's truck and continued with cleaning and storing the food that was leftover - which wasn't much. Tonya never thanked Matteo and Elena for taking care of all the food and cleaning, she didn't appreciate anything that was done for her, it was never enough.

It was time to cut the cake. As Billy hollered for everyone to gather round the cake his purposeful steps positioned to gain balance made the crowd cringe in fear he was going to land on the cake. Tonya and Billy sliced the cake and thankfully didn't smash it in one another's faces, just ate it with their fingers and then Billy sucked the frosting off Tonya's fingers. That was enough to ruin anyone's appetite. Anita cut the cake and served the slices to the guests with the help of Angelo and Anthony. The boys were having a great time staying up later than usual, eating cake and playing with the bocce ball.

The guests spent a reasonable amount of time at the party, enjoyed their dinner, music and games, then said their goodbyes offering their best wishes to the bride and groom. There was still alcohol so there was still Roger, Billy, and Tonya. Artie ordered a cab to come pick them up as Anita and Elena finished cleaning up after the guests. Matteo and Dominic took down all the tables and stacked them along with the chairs as Tonya and Billy snuggled with Roger sitting uncomfortably close to them. The cab arrived; the party was over.

Anthony and Angelo fell asleep in the spare room and Grandpa Artie insisted they not wake them said that Anita and Matteo can go home and rest. Sounded like a great plan. As Matteo and Anita said their goodbyes to Dominic and Elena, Artie and Helen readied for bed. It was a great day but an exhausting day and everyone was ready for a good night's sleep. Except for Dominic and Elena.

They weren't ready to say goodbye, so they sat on a blanket on the lawn next to the stacked tables and chairs. Dominic talked about everything including how painful it was to lose his mom when he was just 7 years old. He mentioned his mom on their first date, but this time he went into greater detail telling Elena how he remembered going into her room and seeing her with no hair. How her frail arms gave the strongest hugs, her eyes could melt the coldest of hearts.

His mom suffered from breast cancer. His dad, Dante, never remarried saying Mary was his wife and there would never be another. He was attractive and women were interested he jokingly insisted Mary would haunt him if he ever dated another woman. Dante worked as an Engineer with a chemical plant he was a good, hard-working man, always smiling and happy. Planning to retire in the next year Dante planned to visit "the old country" to see relatives he hasn't seen in more than 10 years.

Dominic and Elena talked and talked and before they knew it the sun was coming up and they weren't even tired. Sadly, it was time for Dominic to say goodbye while Elena quietly snuck into the house as not to wake anyone.

How was Elena still not tired? Filled with thoughts of Dominic made it difficult to fall asleep, yet somehow at some point Elena drifted off to sleep only to wake up to Anthony and Angelo crawling into her bed. Elena reached for the remote and put on whatever cartoon she could find. They snuggled as Elena tried to grab a bit more sleep.

The boys were hungry, and they knew no one made better breakfast than Auntie Elena. Elena was dragging and so sleepy but thinking about why she was so sleepy made her smile. Dominic. She was jealous thinking he probably got to sleep in because he didn't have to work today.

It's 8 am and Elena is just starting to gather up breakfast ingredients when there's a knock on the door. It's Dominic with an armful of breakfast. Can this man be any more perfect? Dominic handed off the bag of muffins and breakfast sandwiches to the boys who ran the goodies to grandma and grandpa so quickly they didn't even say thank you. Dominic then headed back to the car to return with 6 lattes. The boys, Artie and Helen enjoyed the delicious breakfast as Elena enjoyed a second latte - hey, she didn't get any sleep! Now with their full bellies the boys hugged "Uncle Dom" and thanked him several times.

Dominic had the day off work and he and Elena planned to spend the day together. After a quick shower Elena threw on shorts and a tank top grabbed up her nephews, dropped them off at Matteo and Anita's house with the leftover breakfast then she and Dominic headed off to his home.

Even after two lattes, Elena was still ready for a nap. She and Dominic lay in his huge bed where they've done just about everything but sleep and nodded off. Snuggled up to this amazing man was the most comforting feeling in the world.

It wasn't until nearly 5pm when Elena woke up. Leaving Dominic in the bed to rest Elena scrounged up what food she can find in Dominic's bachelor kitchen and made a pasta dish with tomatoes, cheese, and a drizzle of olive oil. Simple and delicious. Oh and of course wine. Dominic is a closet sommelier - his wine selection is impeccable.

Elena showered again after dinner and Dominic insisted, he too needed another shower and joined her. After watching a movie and enjoying a few more glasses of wine, the two snuggled back into bed and called it a night. Morning always comes too quickly. Dominic had to get to work, Elena stayed in bed watching him get into his uniform. Dominic kissed her goodbye and headed off to work. Elena lay in bed for a bit longer then begrudgingly got out to get her day started. Elena did some laundry, dishes then headed home.

While we learned through Tonya that Jean had two more babies, Tonya and Billy struggled to get pregnant. Tonya blaming Billy's excessive marijuana smoking and Billy blaming Tonya for sleeping around so much said her uterus was probably too tired to make a baby. Tonya never liked children, but Billy wanted a "junior" and was insisting she better figure out how to give him a baby. Tonya told him to get a dog. For the dog's sake, please No!

A baby for Tonya just wasn't in the cards. She and Billy continued to just get by, always with a beer in hand no matter what time of day. Tonya made weekly visits to see her mom, and it wasn't until Artie finally looked in the checkbook that he realized why Tonya was always visiting. She was borrowing money. Well, not borrowing, she never paid it back, she was getting $200 a week from Helen. Tonya claimed it was for cleaning their already clean home.

Artie knew they could afford to give her the money so he really didn't complain that Helen was giving Tonya $800 a month, he didn't like it, but he never complained he believed Billy wasn't working and wanted to make sure they could afford their home. If he did mention anything to Helen, she would become upset saying she was trying to help her daughter.

He didn't like that Tonya always took advantage of Helen and he could see how manipulative she was but giving her some extra money may ensure she doesn't come back home. Why Helen allowed Tonya to take advantage of her is what troubled Artie most. His wife should be treated respectfully and with love, there was no reason for her to be treated poorly by anyone.

A few weeks later during one of Tonya's visits, Artie couldn't catch himself in time and asked, "here for your weekly paycheck?" Tonya was furious and said he better hope that he dies before Helen because no one is going to want to take care of him – WHO SAYS THAT?! She was just evil. Her tone towards Artie has never been pleasant but now she went out of her way to be hurtful towards him.

Artie never told Helen about Tonya's remarks not wanting to further burden Helen but now that Helen was recovering from her second stroke and used a walker to get around, he did his best to keep any negative comments, thoughts, or actions away from his wife. Her vision was beginning to fade, and she was diagnosed with macular degeneration. He cherished his wife and took great care to make certain she was always comfortable.

Tonya never asked about her health or how she was doing. If it wasn't about Tonya she just wasn't interested. She complained to Helen that a coworker at the bank called her "cold-hearted" and that Billy says she's not fat so if anyone tells Helen otherwise, they're lying. She would defend herself against possible future insults that never came to fruition because no one cared enough to talk about her. Being called cold-hearted was however, spot on. Tonya didn't explain why the coworker called her that but was very upset about it as she attempted to explain the coworker's jealousy to Helen as the reason behind the name-calling.

Tonya gathered up her paycheck, one of the necklaces and a watch Helen had on her side table then made her way out the door. Always taking. Just a horrible person. If she needed money, she knew Helen would give it to her – Tonya would take the money is more like it, she wrote out the check for whatever amount and would even sign Helen's name which she mastered over the years.

Now that she knew Artie looked over the checking account, she attempted to be a bit more discreet so stealing her mother's jewelry for extra beer money was the easy route.

Elena's room was locked so that was upsetting for Tonya who had hoped to rustle up more treasures to pawn. She came over weekly, so Artie reminded Elena to keep her door locked at all times. He knew Tonya was a bad person and didn't trust her around Helen or the house. Knowing this, she tried to make her visits to Helen when Artie wasn't home. If Matteo's truck was in the driveway she'd drive by until he left, Matteo was smart enough to know she was up to no good.

Elena came home with a delicious meal for her parents. As she helped Helen to her favorite chair, she set out the dinner and detailed the meal Helen was about to enjoy. Artie barely sat down before he started enjoying the pasta with shrimp and broccoli in a light cream sauce and fresh bread.

Meals from Elena were the highlight of Helen's day. She was always certain to bring enough for the two of them to enjoy for lunch the following day. Elena filled their freezer with various soups and prepped meals that they can have at any time. Artie said they had enough food to last them a year, yet never turned down a fresh delicious dinner from her.

Elena was a great daughter, she, taking care of their food and chores, Matteo taking care of the house repairs and lawn work. They didn't plan it to be this way, it just happened it's what family does. They both loved being with their parents, so it wasn't a chore for them to take care of their needs. Artie would think to himself this is what he always wanted. Good kids, loving wife, nice home. He wondered if they didn't have the two girls if Matteo and Elena would still be so perfect. He felt guilty thinking such things, the two girls gave him nothing, but grief and heartache and he knew it was more damaging how they treated Helen and that bothered him more than anything.

Looking for the positives in his children, Jean was living with her man and had a few kids of her own, there didn't seem to be too much drama with her other than her not working. Tonya's held the bank job for quite some time and is now married to Billy and they seem happy. He didn't care whether they had a lot of money he just wanted everyone to be happy. If his kids were all happy it would make for Helen to be happier.

He never had to worry about Matteo and Elena they always had a focus of what they were going to do and what was expected of them. Artie knew they would both be successful in whatever they decided to do. Now that Matteo was an Electrician, had a beautiful wife, handsome well-behaved sons, and a great home, it was Elena's turn. Artie was excited for Elena's life to flourish.

It was obvious from early childhood Elena's passion for food would be a big part of her life and now she hoped Dominic would also be a big part of her life forever. Dominic was coming to over to pick up Elena he planned to make her dinner. He said he learned enough to impress her with his culinary prowess. Elena wasn't sure he knew how to cook or what he could cook so she jokingly brought along a bottle of antacids.

Dominic unlocked the door and Elena walked in to see dozens and dozens of tulip bouquets, her favorite flower. She turned to look at him and he was on one knee with the cheesiest grin she couldn't help but laugh. "Stop it...Let me do this" Dominic insisted.

His proposal was heartfelt and his hand trembled as he slid the ring onto her finger. Elena didn't even notice the ring she was so immersed in this handsome man. "So you're not making dinner?" Elena teased. Dominic ordered Chinese, opened a bottle of wine, and sat with his fiancée. The ring was stunning, a 1.5 carat diamond stud set on a stunning white gold band.

They've been together nearly 4 years, so Artie and Helen were expecting a proposal would happen soon. Artie was more than happy to give Dominic his blessing. When the phone rang Artie was quick to answer with "yessss???" Elena knew he knew and just laughed. The wedding was just two months later. Elena, Dominic, Matteo, Anita, Dante, Artie, Helen, and Elena's nephews went to Florida for a beach wedding. No, Tonya and Jean were not invited, this was a special day that was not to be ruined by haters.

Dominic was handsomely dressed in a blue fitted suit adorned with a yellow tulip (of course) corsage comfortably placed in his lapel, a crisp white shirt, and brown shoes. Elena's dress was a sheath silhouette that gracefully highlighted her tone body, her hair down with strands effortlessly framing her lovely face. It was a beach wedding so Elena opted for a soft sandal that would be sand friendly.

Matteo and Anita were the best man/maid of honor. Artie cried as he handed his daughter off to Dominic then Dante got up and hugged Artie thanking him for allowing Elena to become a part of his family. Dante was genuine and kind, fit right in with the family. Helen was seated with Angelo and Anthony on either side then joined by Artie and Dante. After the ceremony too many photos were taken. The boys were getting restless and hungry.

Time for an expensive seafood dinner at a restaurant that also offered macaroni and cheese – the boys' favorite meal. When the lobster arrived, Matteo quipped "Hey just like Tonya's wedding" they all laughed as Helen reminded them that Tonya's wedding dinner was delicious and just as good. Artie stated "Of course it was, Elena and Matteo made it" Helen said "That's what I meant" adding a small chuckle. The champagne flowed; the kisses endless. Matteo, Dante, and Artie took turns giving heart-felt and sometimes embarrassing speeches about the newlyweds then Dominic gave his speech. Tears flowed as Dominic talked about his mother's love and how he knew she selected Elena to be his wife. It was a beautiful moment.

Elena wanted to invite her aunts, uncles and cousins, being a destination wedding felt it wasn't fair to ask anyone to spend money for her wedding she also insisted on no gifts. They all sent cards and gifts because that's the kind of people they were, always giving and kind.

Dominic and Elena spent a week alone in Florida after their families left. The honeymoon could have been anywhere since they barely left the room. Elena insisted they had to do a few touristy things – one day they went on an airboat ride and another day they went on a sunset cruise. They had a great time just being together uninterrupted, but it was time to head home. Elena filled out thank you cards on the plane ride home insisting Matteo add something to each of the cards which he did without complaining.

Things quickly fell into place. Moving into Dominic's place was an easy transition. They bought new furniture had a few rooms painted and after a few weeks they were done with the home renovations life was great.

Elena was making her usual stop by her parents to bring over dinner. Artie had a sneaky look to him and told her he had a big surprise and she needed to be there by 3:00 the next afternoon. Elena tried to guess what it could be, "You're making fritole?" (Delicious Italian donuts with raisins, lemon, and orange zest, as kids Elena and Matteo couldn't get enough) We're going on vacation?" Artie just laughed and told her to be there at 3:00 to find out. Artie loved silly surprises it was usually just an excuse to see Dominic and Elena more often.

Always early, Elena arrived home at 2:27. I don't smell fritole…where's my surprise? Artie and Helen were ready to go, go where? Artie grabbed his truck keys and said "Let's go". Okay… This will be fun. They were taking Artie's pickup truck, so Helen squeezed in the middle and Elena got in excited to see where they were headed.

As Artie pulled up to the spot where the Dasker family's gas station used to be, Artie exclaimed "We're here!" looking around at the now empty lot "We're where?" asked Elena. "You're restaurant!" Helen excitedly shouted.

Artie and Helen purchased the vacant property as a graduation/wedding gift for Elena and Dominic. Artie told her it would be a perfect spot for a restaurant, he assured Elena, he got it at a great price because the lot had been vacant for so long and he "knew a guy". Hugging her parents before they even got out of the truck Helen started crying she was so happy.

Matteo and Anita pulled up knowing about the surprise. Matteo joked "Hope this doesn't cut into Tonya's paychecks" Helen pretended not to hear, Artie laughed and Elena seriously said, "I hope not, that'll be trouble for me!" Matteo laughed.

A million thoughts were running through her head about what she was going to do, what kind of restaurant, how much would this cost, could she actually do this? Artie said "Let's check it out". She quickly called Dominic and told him to come see their wedding gift. Dominic was already on his way. Of course, Artie cleared the purchase with Dominic first.

Dominic thanked Artie and Helen for their generosity more times than necessary. He agreed this was a great area for a restaurant. It was in the center of town, close to everything. As they all looked at the vacant lot it was time for Helen and Artie to head home and told Matteo they are going to keep the boys overnight, so they didn't have to rush home. Artie waited in Matteo's driveway for the school bus to bring the boys home. As they got off the bus they were thrilled to see grandpa. It was always a good time when they spent it with grandpa.

Anita was thrilled to have an impromptu date night. Matteo suggested the four of them go out for a nice dinner to celebrate. Dominic joked "well, the restaurant isn't even built yet!" Matteo agreed Elena's restaurant would provide the best food anywhere, but he was hungry now. They went out for pizza and beer – dinner doesn't always have to be expensive to be good and it's really the company that makes the meal that much better.

They were discussing ideas of what kind of restaurant would fit in their town, what was missing, what clientele they would want too many questions and plans. Everyone had ideas to offer, they also knew Elena has always dreamt of this, so her restaurant ideas were probably already solidified. But now that it's coming to fruition, those dreams must be brought to life.

Elena had to conceptualize what type of restaurant she would want. First step was to get her friend Anna involved. Anna is an architect and has been friends with Elena since 1st grade. One thing Elena knew is what the name would be "Cibo" which translates to "food" in English. Simple.

Elena gave Anna some ideas of what she envisioned, and Anna got right to work. Matteo insisted on doing all the electrical work, which saved a ton of money. Artie could do any concrete work that was needed, and Dominic dabbled in carpentry and was the muscle of the bunch - anything that needed to be moved, pulled, dragged, lifted, Dominic was the guy.

Every time Elena walked into the restaurant, she fell more and more in love with it. Artie did a masterful job on the floors. Concrete but he stamped the concrete to look like real wood floors. Great for longevity and easy cleaning. The floors continued to a small outdoor space where Artie built a corner fountain.

The fountain was nearly 10 feet tall surrounded by fig trees and small boxwood shrubs. The outdoor tables were faux wood draped with crisp white linens to match the interior look. It was probably the quickest a restaurant has ever been created from concept to completion.

The outdoor chairs were wooden folding chairs, yet really comfortable. Seating outdoors was limited to 25 with the option for the restaurant to leave the wall of glass accordion patio doors open for the guests indoor to enjoy the weather as well.

The inside of the restaurant was a hug of comfort the moment you step inside you feel at home in the spacious reception area with two sofas and an oak desk with a high back chair where the hostess greets the guests.

Four large wooden round tables with seating for 8 created a strong center of the restaurant, four tables line the left and four tables to the right each providing seating for four. Just beyond the dining tables are the lovely accordion patio doors with the natural light flowing through the restaurant it looked light a painting. The bar was on the right of the accordion doors, it was a large bar with 16 handsome bar stools.

The ceiling was an open ceiling painted black. Matteo installed lighting that made it look as though you sat under the stars while dining. He also installed back lights on the bar that showed off the selections of liquor and beautiful lighting to showcase the wine dispensing system, it stored the wine at its optimal temperature the wine was easy to dispense by just pressing the lever.

There was something even more special behind the bar - a glass case with soft lighting, inside the case was the rock that Champ had gifted to Elena and resting on top the stuffed toy from her childhood friend David. Matteo had the case made knowing it would be a perfect inclusion to the restaurant. Elena could show the world the precious gifts from two of her best friends. Matteo's thoughtfulness meant the world to Elena. He was working so hard on the restaurant and still had time to think to do something so amazing.

To the right of the entrance was the kitchen it was well lit and inviting, Matteo didn't cut any corners and did a fabulous job. It was an open concept where the diners can see the creation of their dinners. In the right corner were the restrooms with two solid entry doors for better separation from the restaurant and guests.

Elena didn't like a lot of clutter, so the walls were adorned with beautiful photos that alternated between Italian architecture including the Leaning Tower of Pisa, The Pantheon, Doge's Place, Norman Palace, and photos that Anita took of beautifully plated foods when they went on their honeymoon to Europe. Anita felt like a celebrity having her photos hanging on the walls.

Elena unveiled a huge surprise for Artie. Above the kitchen area was a large intricately framed photo of Artie and Helen with photos of her grandparents on either side next to those were photos of Dominic's parents and grandparents. Elena said that Artie always encouraged her cooking, taking her to his mom's house to cook teaching her so much about food she wanted to honor him by displaying the photos. This was one of Artie's proudest moments.

It was time to prepare for a soft opening and invite her friends and family to give the restaurant a trial run. It was a Thursday night; Elena did this knowing Dominic didn't have to work on Friday and it was important her husband be there as it was just as much his restaurant as it was hers. Elena wanted the whole family to own the restaurant but Artie insisted he gifted each of his children the same amount of money and they used it as they saw fit. Rather than give Elena money, he purchased the property insisting everyone was treated fairly. Matteo agreed saying Elena needed to quit worrying about everyone else and take care of her dream. It was her turn.

Thankfully May's weather cooperated it was a lovely evening the weather was just slightly cool with hints of a warm whisper of wind. The heat lamps on the patio were put on low so guests could comfortably sit outdoors. The accordion doors were open halfway which allowed the evening breezes to softly rustle the table linens.

The kitchen was bustling prepping for the evening crowd with the sous chef dicing, chopping, and readying the ingredients, the kitchen staff all anxious to get working. Elena was cooking most of the dishes, leaving dessert up to Diana who eagerly accepted a position working for Elena. They met in culinary school and became fast friends.

Dominic's dad, Dante, a few aunts, uncles, and cousins along several of his police officer friends, began to fill the restaurant. Elena's friends mingled with everyone as they arrived, Matteo and Anita were behind the bar assisting the two bartenders filling ice, making certain everything was in its place. Anthony and Angelo were on the outside patio with Helen and Artie they were enjoying a charcuterie board loaded with cheeses, sausages, olives, and peppers.

There were several charcuterie boards strategically placed throughout the restaurant for the guests to enjoy while the appetizers as main courses were being prepared.

Dominic was in the kitchen watching Elena work so happily. He was in awe watching her handle every aspect of the kitchen so effortlessly. He waited patiently for Elena to take a break so he can steal a quick kiss and hand her a glass of wine knowing he shouldn't interrupt her work flow she was in her zone. Elena glanced up seeing her handsome man insisted she was done working, trusting her sous chef and staff could handle the kitchen from this point, she tenderly smooched with Dominic then went out to greet her guests.

As Elena greeted her guests, she was happy that everyone she invited was showing up, everyone of course except for Tonya and

Billy. Helen tried to convince Tonya to come telling her the food and drinks were free so why not just come for dinner? Free drinks excited Billy, but Tonya refused to go. Seems Helen spent most of her time attempting to convince Tonya to join the family. As for Jean, there was no way to get a hold of her as Tonya refused to tell Helen her phone number or address. Jean still hasn't talked with Artie, Helen, or her other siblings in years. Just Tonya.

Artie's twin sisters Giana and Maria arrived. They're the loveliest ladies in the world and Elena and Matteo were very close to them. Anytime there was a gathering, Giana, Maria, and their families were always on the guest list. Their children and husbands were all very kind, generous, and ready with a glass of wine and too much food every time you'd visit. Elena and Matteo were close with their cousins too and shared many laughs and memories. Anytime they got together with Artie's side of the family the laughs were endless, the food abundant and the love overflowing.

Elena's cousin, Andrew and his bleach-blonde wife entered and bee-lined to Helen. They never cared for the "Italians" as they would refer to Artie's side of the family. Andrew is Helen's nephew closer to Helen's age than to Elena's. His face was showing his age and his body was beginning to look frail and his eyes shady as ever. There were stories about Andrew stealing all his brothers' inheritance. He told his siblings he would take care of their dying father; they signed off on documents without reading them and he kept all the money. Artie had no doubt that is exactly what happened.

Andrew was quite a douche, as his brothers referred to him. They rarely spoke and weren't close as children, sort of like the relationship Elena had with her sisters. After the death of his father his brothers refused to speak to him which made the rest of the family believe he really did take all his parents' money. Family. Helen was very fond of Andrew for whatever reason maybe she was just too trusting, or it could be she didn't really have any other family since her brother and sister-in-law passed away.

Artie didn't care for Andrew or his wife, saying his wife Martha was a tramp and Andrew a thief – never to their faces, Artie was always kind to Andrew because it was all the family

Helen had left since her other two nephews lived out of State. Andrew ended up with Martha after Andrew's brother dumped her. They have a daughter...maybe...there were always whispers about the paternity. Everyone had a "Moment with Martha" so chances were good Andrew wasn't the father. Everyone has something in their family. Right? Artie stepped over to Matteo and whispered, "Andrew's here, watch the silverware" and they both laughed, Anita overhearing this said "No Joke. We should!" they laughed again.

Dominic's friends and Elena's friends hit it off and Dominic was so proud to discuss his wine selections and their preferred pairings. Elena and Dominic were so pleased to see his friends and her friends getting along so well, even looked as though there may be some romance in the air. Anna was still single and wasn't dating anyone at this point, so Elena was sure to introduce her to every single friend of Dominic's. They were all having a great time. The room was loud with laughter shadowed by Dean Martin songs playing just above a soft conversation.

The guests were seated indoors, Angelo and Anthony wanted to stay outdoors so Anita and Matteo sat at the tables nearest the patio, turned up the heat on the heat lamps and the boys continued to enjoy the charcuterie board, Italian sodas and Diana made them both a special dessert saying it was okay to enjoy before dinner because it's a special night. The boys were always so well-behaved, "Little Matteo's" is what Artie would call them. They were always well-mannered boys, and everyone adored them.

As the guests were seated with their full wine glasses or beverage of choice, the wait staff brought out several appetizers served family style. As the appetizer plates were cleared off, glasses topped off and the crumbs wiped off, the entrées made it to the tables quickly. As guests enjoyed their dinners the restaurant almost fell silent. The food was being so enjoyed the chatter almost subsided. Diana's tiramisu, espresso and lattes rounded out the evening.

Elena thanked everyone for coming, gave a sincere speech about her appreciation to her parents, husband, brother, sister-in-law and all her family. She added an extra congratulations to her husband for being promoted Lieutenant as the crowd cheered and clapped Dominic blushed and ordered in jest for them to stop making a fuss causing his buddies whoop and cheer a bit louder. As belts were loosened, drinks were finished, and sighs of full bellies hummed across the restaurant it was a successful night that was reaching its end.

The guests soon made their way out of the restaurant Elena told Dominic her arms were going to fall off from so many hugs. It was an evening of celebration, family, and love.

The restaurant opened to rave reviews. The local paper did a story on the restaurant which brought even more guests to the already booming restaurant. Artie would just come and hang out at the restaurant, doing anything he could to be of use. Oftentimes Artie would meet with Dante or bring in a friend for dinner, Elena's treat of course. Artie never ordered, Elena would surprise Artie, Dante, and their friends with her dinner selection. Everything was absolutely great.

Dominic was doing great at work, Dante retired and headed to "the old country" where he planned to spend a few months, Artie was retired, taking care of Helen, enjoying his grandsons, and spending his spare time at the restaurant.

After two years the restaurant continued to be busier than most. Elena and Dominic were there every day. The restaurant only served dinner, so their days were filled with getting the restaurant prepped, visiting Helen and Artie, going to her nephews school for whatever performance they had and enjoying her alone time with Dominic.

Things were just about to become more great...Never being pregnant before, Elena just knew. Dominic was over the moon when she showed him the test results. Artie and Helen were thrilled and Matteo said "It's about time". Elena had a very easy pregnancy wasn't hindered with morning sickness and thanks to healthy eating and her regular exercise routine gained just 22 pounds and was back to her tone self in just a few months.

Their first baby Alexandria was a joy, lovely pale skin, light eyes and effortless. Artie fell in love with this sweet angel claiming she had the same demeanor Elena had as a baby, just full of sweetness. A hotter than usual summer day welcomed baby number 2. Bella was a mirror image of Elena with her olive skin, dark eyes and dark hair, she too was a great baby with a sweet disposition. The restaurant and two babies kept Dominic and Elena busy, but it was a good busy. Life was beautiful.

Tonya hated that Elena had children. She and Billy were never blessed with children which in hindsight was a blessing in itself. Some people should not procreate, and Tonya was a perfect example of someone who should never be trusted to care for something so precious. Tonya continued to collect her weekly paychecks from Helen and took every opportunity to make up stories about Elena and Matteo, speak ill of them, anything she can say or do to create a divide between Helen and her other children. Tonya loved throwing in tidbits about Jean and how awful her life was saying she heard that Jean had given up several babies for adoption. Tonya took joy in filling her mother's mind and heart with sadness. She is just evil.

Tonya was also jealous that Elena had a good relationship with their dad. This always infuriated her and probably fueled her dislike for him. Artie often talked about Elena's children not intentionally trying to hurt Tonya, he just couldn't help but the rave about how wonderful the girls were. Tonya's visits were timed to when she knew Artie would be leaving so she would have little to no interaction with him. Artie would meet Elena and the girls at the restaurant, enjoy a nice breakfast as he kept an eye on the girls while Elena did paperwork, payroll and all the busy work that needed to be done.

Artie enjoyed picking up the girls now that they were toddlers, and he didn't have to change diapers. So after their morning meet-up at the restaurant he would take the girls on adventures. They had many trips to the zoo, park, anywhere he could show them off. The girls were very attached to their grandpa and looked forward to his daily visits.

After a few years Dominic said "Let's have another" it was that easy. Elena loved children, loved being a mom and Dominic was a great dad always involved in everything they were doing, from storytelling, making blanket forts or surprising Elena with fresh baked cookies, he couldn't hear "daddy" enough.

Theodore too was born on a hot summer day looking like a perfect blend of Elena and Dominic. His precious face blessed by angels, his full head of dark hair the envy of grown men, and his sweet disposition just like his sisters. Elena and Dominic were very lucky to have such relaxed babies they weren't about to risk their good fortune being blessed with three children was enough. They're family was complete.

Tonya's hatred, if possible, grew even more. How dare Elena have another baby so effortlessly when Tonya couldn't have *one*! Billy begging for a child stopped after a bit and he seemed okay with not having any children. Perhaps Tonya drilled it into his now bald head that they didn't need any kids. She had a power over Billy and was able to convince him of what he wanted or didn't want.

As Elena's children grew, so did their kindness, all sweet, happy and loved being at the restaurant. Elena loved that her children were close with one another and were visited often by Anita, Matteo, and their sons. Dominic would hold class to teach his daughters, Theodore, Angelo, and Anthony self-defense saying it was important to be able to protect yourself at all times. These lessons often ended in tickle fights.

Theodore was four years old, and the girls were in elementary school. Elena decided to hire more employees so who better to hire than her amazing nephews - Matteo's sons started working at the restaurant, they were busboys, dishwashers, and even helped in the kitchen.

Elena's pastry chef Diana brought in her friend to meet Elena and hopefully get a job. With Diana's recommendation Johnnie was hired on the spot. Elena had a full staff of wonderful employees, the help of her nephews and Artie she had more than enough help and would find herself being near boredom at times.

Artie making his usual stop at the restaurant wasn't so "usual" this time, this time it came with a surprise. Hurriedly rushing

Elena out the front door as she cuddled Theodore she was quickly greeted by Dominic and the girls with their new friend – a puppy!

Artie's friend came through with yet another 'full-blooded' German shepherd pup. Oh the baby looked so much like Champ. Theodore squeezed the pup as Dominic put his hand between the pup and Theodore so he didn't squeeze too hard. The girls squealed in delight at their mom's joy. Dominic's only complaint is that it was a girl, he joked he had hoped to add more testosterone to the household. Dominic loved dogs, his K-9 passed away just before he was promoted to Lieutenant and this little lady brought back of flood of great memories.

Everyone was eager to play with and train Ladybug, as named by Alexandria. She was quick to learn and so pleased to show off new tricks. Matteo never got another dog, just farm animals so he came over with a basket full of toys and treats for the new pup. He also supplied the restaurant with fresh eggs from his chickens and would bring in bags of vegetables from his garden.

Growing quickly Ladybug was allowed to visit the restaurant but had to stay on the enclosed patio with Artie and the children. Artie built a beautiful area for Ladybug to relax and created a secluded area for Ladybug to 'do her business' far away from the guest area. Elena would drop the kids off at school then take Ladybug to the restaurant with her while she took care of the administrative work. Dominic would pick her up in the early afternoon from the restaurant so she can be trained by himself and the K-9 team. It was just an excuse for him to spend time with her, she was such a smart dog.

Angelo was 18 and Anthony 17, they were as tall as Matteo and just as handsome. Dominic enjoyed having his nephews work at the restaurant and looked forward to the day his kids would be working alongside him and Elena. The family was always helping at the restaurant, it was like a second home. Angelo was taking college courses wanting to be an Electrician like his dad, Anthony was heading into his senior year at high school. There was no set schedule for them to work, they came in when they could and worked as long as they wanted. Even with that kind of freedom they were probably the hardest workers in the restaurant.

Elena had everything. A popular restaurant, beautiful children, handsome husband, a goofy dog, and a lovely home. She and Dominic worked hard for everything they have. Artie always told his children work hard and you'll have a good life. Be lazy and life will pass you by. When life is passing by oftentimes it goes unnoticed until it's too late. Tonya's life-long jealousy was unfounded. She had every opportunity Matteo and Elena had yet for whatever reason she defied happiness, ignored circumstances that would have bettered her and had zero drive to improve her life.

Artie recognized Matteo and Elena and their hard work. He was so proud of them and all they have accomplished. Not because they were both married to wonderful people, had great kids, and successful, but rather they were good people. They were kind, thoughtful and filled with love and that was something he always prayed for all of his children.

Tonya owned her ignorance, wearing it as a badge of honor. Delusional to believe she had achieved a goal to be prideful of, as she continued to share stories about Jean to Helen. Her anger fueled by anyone that she perceived was better than her, her jealousy inflated her desire to make others suffer and fail.

Every now and again Helen made the mistake of sharing some of Tonya's made-up stories with Artie. He was kind enough to understand Helen's pain from hearing such stories doing his best to set her mind and heart at ease he would tell her Tonya was joking, laughing, and telling her it was okay, and was sure Tonya was just kidding. Although Helen felt Artie was just trying to make her feel better, she let him believe that it had and would smile and agree with him.

Tonya's envy was evident to all around her, Helen seemed oblivious to her bitterness and anger or just chose to believe her daughter wasn't so filled with hate. Helen refrained from mentioning Elena's name in front of Tonya, she almost feared the extent of Tonya's anger. Once Helen accidentally mentioned the restaurant and Tonya screamed at her to "Quit talking about that bitch! You always talk about her!" she frightened Helen, who quickly apologized and changed the subject. She knew to be quiet and agreeable with Tonya, being frightened of her own child it was something she would share with no one.

As much as Helen wanted to share stories about Elena, Matteo, and their families she couldn't. Not even to Andrew, her nephew, he even seemed miffed when they were mentioned. It was all odd to Helen why there was such spite on the part of Tonya and Andrew. They would both become aggressive and defensive with Helen whenever she talked about anyone but the two of them. They were mean to Helen, yet she continued to include them in her life, continued to love them and give them whatever they asked for, mostly money.

She wondered why the two of them having nothing in common were oddly close. Thinking it was nice that Tonya was close to someone in the family, Tonya told her she just doesn't like the "Italians" that Helen's people were so much better. For whatever reason the "we don't like the Italians" became their thing. No reason for it, Artie's family were the ones who always stepped up to help, listen, give, if you were in need, they were there.

Artie's heart would break if he saw how they treated her and how it affected his loving wife he would have probably called in a few favors from his buddies so it's probably good he didn't know how depraved they were. All she ever did was to try to be a good mom she did nothing wrong. Being proud of your child shouldn't anger others, a parent should be allowed to show pride without a threat of being mistreated.

Artie would take Helen to the restaurant to visit the kids, Ladybug, and to enjoy time away from the house. She loved sitting on the patio at the restaurant by the water fountain while Ladybug rested on her feet. She bragged to everyone within earshot that her husband built the beautiful fountain. On occasion Helen would enjoy a glass of wine on the restaurant patio soaking in the beauty listening to the quiet bustling within the restaurant. Artie would "work" around the restaurant and bring Helen out an array of foods prepared by Elena and her staff. Helen snuck treats to Ladybug, she thought she was sneaking the treats, but Ladybug's attentiveness often gave it away.

Angelo and Anthony were now helping in the kitchen and were quick to run grandma over their creations. They were pleased with their newfound cooking skills and grandma and grandpa were delighted to taste them. Turning up the patio heaters made it too comfortable, and Helen nodded off. She was gently awoken by Artie who said he was ready to go home, she insisted on staying a bit longer. Artie brought out a couple of bowls of soup and after their soup Elena packed them up some goodies to take with them.

Fall was just around the corner which meant it was time for Matteo's famous clambake. The family looks forward to his yearly bake. The restaurant was fully staffed, and all the family gathered at Matteo's. He never just had clams. A party at Matteo's was massive. More than 45 relatives and friends had their cars parked across the yard and walked in with treats of their own. Aunts Maria and Giana brought eggplant parmesan (their specialty), other relatives brought desserts and side dishes. Elena just brought wine and beer, it was the one time she didn't cook anything.

Matteo had a 40-pound hunk of beef on the spit that smelled like heaven; huge pots on propane burners for the hundreds of clams; corn and potatoes on the grill, everything was amazing as usual. Dominic and Elena had several friends at the clambake, they've been enjoying the bakes for years now. The growing number of kids was so great to see friends that had babies, relatives that had babies, kids were everywhere.

Matteo gave the kids bags of carrots to feed to the goats, Ladybug had one too, he had volleyball, bocce ball, all sorts of games for everyone to enjoy. His parties were always the best. Ladybug was in the barn making friends with the goats as the kids made the introductions. Ladybug was a gentle dog; the goats just weren't interested.

The families and friends all got along there was infinite laughter, jokes, stories, these were the best of times. Matteo set up several tents for anyone who wanted to spend the night, some even brought their own tents and sleeping bags and gathered around the huge bon fire Matteo had built. Oddly enough he never caught the grass on fire joked Elena.

With full bellies, a star-filled sky and kids that smelled like goats it was time for Elena and Dominic to pack up their family and Ladybug and head home. The kids were so exhausted from all the playing they were asleep before Dominic started the car. The silence was deafened by the overwhelming happiness and love for his family. Dominic always said he is the luckiest man alive and every time he said that Elena agreed wholeheartedly that yes "He is the luckiest man alive" then they would laugh. If ever someone wanted to explain what a family should be, what love is, what goodness is, this was it.

It was early November when the phone rang just after 4:00 a.m. Never good news at that hour. Matteo quickly telling Elena Artie has been rushed to the hospital. The doctor explained to Matteo that Artie had suffered what in laymen terms is referred to as a "Triple A" medical meaning is an abdominal aortic aneurysm he told Matteo after a rupture, chances of survival, are very slim, given Artie's age he was surprised he made it to the hospital and hung on for as long as he had. Matteo was sure his dad was waiting for Elena.

Elena hastened to get ready, Dominic stayed home the children obviously were still sleeping and they thought it best not to wake them. Arriving at the hospital in time for her father's last breaths, Matteo comforted Helen as Anita quietly wept. Elena held her father's hand thanking him for giving her such a beautiful life. Artie's tender squeeze of her hand timed with his last breath. Elena didn't move, just stared until Anita came up and hugged her pulling her from the bedside. The tears fell silently without processing the pain the heart was enduring.

The sadness was palpable. It was always too soon to lose her father Elena still needed Artie, he shouldn't be gone. Matteo's eyes welled with tears as his voice had a calming reassurance as he spoke to Helen. The hospital staff allowed them to wait for the other family members so they can finish their goodbyes.

Tonya was called but didn't show up. It didn't benefit her to be there. Tonya was excited to tell Jean the news. Jean didn't make it to the hospital either. Aunts Maria and Giana and their families came to the hospital, a priest prayed over Artie then soon after the nurse motioned to Matteo that it was time to go. She offered sincere sympathy to the family they were grateful for her kindness and gentle way with Artie. Matteo helped his mom out of the hospital and took her to his home where she slept peacefully in a reclining chair. Dominic and the kids came over to Matteo's, the moment his strong arms wrapped around Elena, she lost it and cried uncontrollably. Dante soon arrived to care for the grandkids as Anita made the necessary phone calls and handled the arrangements. Dante spent as much time at the restaurant as Artie, they became very close friends, so he too was saddened losing his friend. Helen woke in the late afternoon to a warm bowl of soup and a cup of tea.

She was able to eat which was a good thing, Anita sat with her then was joined by the grandkids who snuggled up on the couch next to the recliner. Alexandria and Bella read books as Theodore fell asleep. Just having the grandkids around was comforting to Helen. Angelo and Anthony helped Helen to the restroom so she could freshen up. She wasn't crying just going through the motions. The family came together and comforted one another. Elena was too distraught to help with the funeral planning, Anita, Matteo and Dominic handled everything which gave her yet another reason to love this family, her brother, sister-in-law and husband were so strong, always just a phone call away.

Artie was well-liked more than 100 people came to offer their respects and condolences to Helen. All his buddies were there, all the guys he "knew", they were older, but so charming and full of character. Gus reminding Matteo to come over and make salami "It's what your dad would have wanted" Matteo shook his hand introduced him to Dominic and let him know this was Artie's favorite son-in-law, Gus knew this as he shared many meals with Artie and Dante at Cibo, and was quick to invite Dominic to make salami "It's what your father-in-law would have wanted" Gus was a card, so animated and generous to a fault.

The friends offered hugs, money, stories, whatever they could do to make things a bit easier. Matteo and Anita sitting on either side of Helen introduced the people who came up to console her. Elena, Dominic and their and Matteo's children took up the second row.

Tonya and Billy came just as the service was nearing its end. Jean showed up at the very last minute and was inconsolable. She really put on a show about how she was daddy's girl and how greatly she would miss him. Her boyfriend/husband/fiancé – we never really knew, was there as well. Dominic overheard him bragging about what kind of inheritance they were going to get and how they were going to have a brand-new car sitting in their driveway. Dominic did all he could to refrain from punching in his stupid face just walking away and putting his arm around Elena was all that he needed to do at the moment.

Matteo placed Helen into the waiting limousine to take her to the burial site. Matteo, Anita, Dominic, Elena and all their children joined Helen. Tonya and Billy followed in a pickup truck that he borrowed from a friend. Jean, Conrad and probably a few of their children – the family never met them, piled into a rusty Cadillac as Jean continued her "my daddy" show. To have no sense of humiliation for the absurd behavior was astounding. If it weren't a funeral the show had a chance of being entertaining.

Matteo swore Billy was already drunk after all it was already 10 a.m. The procession began its way to the burial site. As Matteo and Dominic steadied Helen and held her on either side because the walker couldn't be used on the soft, wet ground. Anita and Elena held hands with the children. Tonya encouraged Jean's outrageous show and feigned comforting her as Billy stumbled up, turned around and decided to wait in the truck.

Being a Marine, Artie was given a military funeral with a 21-gun salute. Jean ran up to collect as many spent shells as she could claiming his grandchildren needed something to remember him by. The same grandchildren she never brought over, the same grandchildren that didn't know a thing about Artie or Helen. After the ceremony the mourners headed over to Helen's house for a warm meal prepared of course, by Cibo - Elena's restaurant.

Everyone enjoyed the food as Billy went to fix himself a plate Tonya grabbed him by the arm sternly warning him "Do the right thing, Billy!" he wasn't allowed to eat food prepared by Elena. Tonya refused to eat the food saying it looked disgusting. She was her same old bitchy self. Billy grabbed a couple of beers and headed to the garage to smoke. Nothing like a meal of beer and cigarettes.

Tonya was so bossy no one ever understood what kind of man would put up with her, Matteo believed it was the fact that Tonya supported him as no one ever heard of him actually having a job. Made sense.

Jean cozied up to Helen as she sat on the flowered sofa, and introduced her 4 children; Rainbow, who Helen hadn't seen since she was 4 months old, Leather, Casper, and her son Chambery. Helen was never going to remember any of their names, but she was happy to meet them, they were well-mannered and seemed to really like Helen as they instantly called her grandma.

The introductions continued… At 15 years old, Rainbow had her first baby girl, the baby was with the daddy for the day. Leather was portly and resembled Jean, and Casper was pregnant. Chambery told Helen he wanted to be a bus driver. Jean continued to clamor about her family and how they're all so great and she can't wait for Helen to meet her great-grandchildren.

Jean's chatter and drama appeared to be a welcome albeit theatrical distraction from the sadness. Matteo and Elena checked on her often ensuring Jean wasn't being too intrusive as she talked about her deep love for her daddy and how she is going to miss him the most, that he always liked her best, Helen would nod which Jean believed was affirmation of her bullshit but in actuality Helen's hearing wasn't the best and she refused to wear hearing aids so she may have missed most of the nonsense Jean was spewing.

Matteo asked Elena if she heard about Jean's 62 kids and 127 grandkids. This was this first hint of a laugh from Elena in days.

Matteo hugged her whispering "it's going to be okay, dad had a great life, he loved us, our kids and we all loved him." Tonya seeing Matteo hugging Elena scathingly said to Martha "They're probably sleeping together! What brother hugs his sister?!" Martha lighting yet another cigarette agreed. "Whore" was all she could muddle out between coughs from the cigarette she just inhaled.

Martha pointing out a cousin in a group of mourners and reminding Tonya what "an asshole he is" it was then that Tonya remembered the rumors of Martha pleasuring the cousin's dog. Tonya never missed a beat and loudly questioned, "Wonder if he ever got another dog" Martha knowing exactly what she was referring to, yelled "You're a bitch!" and stormed out of the house. Her moronic husband, Andrew, was quick to shuffle after his skank wife and the two left.

It was a long day for everyone there were so many visitors showing their respect and love for Artie they could have been there for days. Helen was getting visibly tired the house was clearing out, so Elena and Anita got Helen ready for bed. Her elderly face was blanketed in loneliness. Elena gently kissed her forehead and reminded her how loved she is. Anita and Elena sat at end of Helen's bed as she fell asleep in a matter of minutes. She was simply exhausted.

Tonya caught Billy eating a plate of food and hit him upside the head. They left without saying goodbye to anyone.

Artie's sisters Giana and Maria stayed to help Anita and Elena clean the house and wash dishes. Jean tried to talk everyone into letting her spend the night, but Angelo and Anthony were already sleeping in the rooms. The boys wanted to be there for their grandma and make sure she'd be okay. They were very close with their grandfather and wanted to take care of their grandmother. The young men were just as kind as their father.

Jean acting as though she's been slighted left in a huff with her entourage. They were sure to grab up all the leftover food to take with them. Anita, Elena, and their husbands finished up the cleaning, closed the drapes and headed home.

The next morning the boys fixed Helen breakfast and brought her a coffee in bed to see if she was ready to get up. She was in good spirits everything considered. They sat with their grandmother and shared their plans for the day, of doing her yardwork then heading off to the restaurant. Matteo and Anita came in and cleaned up their breakfast dishes, the boys were finishing up the lawn work, and Anita was going to spend the day with Helen.

Helen was fond of Anita she always said she could not have picked a more perfect partner for her son. Helen favored Matteo, understandably. Matteo did everything for Helen even before Artie's passing. Matteo did all their yardwork, handyman jobs, any repairs they needed they would call Matteo. He was quick to help with whatever had to be done. He was a flawless son.

Elena, her children, and Matteo's family were sure to keep Helen busy and visit her often. It was about 2 months after Artie's passing when Jean called saying she had nowhere to live because Conrad was kicking her and the grandkid out of the house she needed to move in with Helen. The family hoped this would be a good thing, someone there to care for Helen 24/7 and they wouldn't have to worry as much.

Jean and granddaughter moved in with Helen. She made her living space in the basement because she said dad would have wanted her to that's where she was when she was pregnant with his beautiful granddaughter – her revisionist history was quite entertaining. The granddaughter was made comfortable in the room next to Helen's.

Tonya would come over and scream at Jean to clean this do that…Helen couldn't see very well so she believed Tonya when she told her that the house was a mess. At one point Tonya was just angry to be angry and started screaming at the little granddaughter. Jean came up and yelled "Is this how you treat Billy's kid? No wonder he's not allowed to see him!" An actual fistfight occurred, there was hair pulling, yelling, luckily Matteo stopped by just in time to break the two beasts apart. He was furious they were behaving this way.

Matteo made Tonya leave and that's when Jean explained Tonya was mad because no one was supposed to know that Billy has a kid with another woman. Oh the scandal. This was the first anyone had heard of Billy having a son. Matteo felt bad that no one had met Billy's son. He was sure the kid would have had a great time hanging out with his boys and Elena's kids. Helen yelled "don't you ever say anything about that son of his again! It's not your business!"

Good news Tonya didn't procreate, and she's not allowed to be around Billy's kid, she isn't a good person and there was no reason to give her the opportunity to influence any living being in any way. Billy a dad? No one knew if he was able to spend time with his son, they hoped he did because he probably would have been a good dad with Tonya involved that wasn't likely.

After a few weeks of calming down, Tonya was stopping by more and more frequently. At one point she brought over three friends to meet Helen. The visit was quick, and after that visit Tonya would stop by weekly with instructions for Jean on what to do with Helen. Jean just listened and pretended that she would obey Tonya's instructions. It was easier than causing another fight in front of Helen. She'd also get her weekly payment – that never stopped. Probably why she kept coming around. Can't pass up those free checks and of course anything of value she could find laying around.

Elena continued to bring over meals for Helen, Jean, and her granddaughter. They were all appreciative and Jean would rave about how delicious the food was probably because she didn't have to cook, and the food was free. Jean, away from Tonya, was pleasant. She thanked Elena every time she brought over food and even made conversation. Matteo's sons would drop off treats and fresh fruits for them as well, stay and visit with their grandmother.

Helen would ask Jean to call Elena to request special dinners and desserts. Elena always included fresh baked bread and if she couldn't get away from the restaurant the boys would be sure to drop it off. Jean told them they didn't have to bring the meals because grandma gave Jean a car so she can come pick up the meals. They said when they're too busy they'll let Jean know, but they enjoy stopping by to see everyone.

As the boys stopped by with one of their deliveries they ran in to Tonya and Billy. Billy grabbed the bag and took a whiff "Roadkill! This has already gone bad, who you looking to poison?!" The boys didn't like Billy, they didn't care for Tonya either. Angelo took the bag back from Billy and said, "It's not for you, there's no squirrel in here" Billy was tempted, but knew not to even think around raising a hand. These boys were big enough to kick his ass effortlessly. Tonya called them little bastards saying they were just like their father. The boys ignored her antagonistic remarks and headed over to their grandmother.

The boys prepped their grandmother for dinner, and she was so excited to dive into the delicious dinner until she heard loudmouth Tonya. She turned the food away saying, "Oh I don't want that, give it to your aunt". The boys were surprised that their grandma didn't want it, Jean told them not to worry she just wasn't allowed to eat the food in front of Tonya. They said there was plenty to share, that wasn't it. Jean told them Tonya is always talking trash and gets really mean when Elena or Matteo is mentioned. So to keep the peace, Helen can't accept the food when Tonya is around.

The boys left the food with Jean telling Anita about what happened with Tonya's awful behavior and her comments to their grandmother and not taking the food. Anita explained a bit about how Tonya was different from their dad and Aunt. She told them a few of the stories from when they were kids but there were so much the boys didn't know about Tonya and her God-awful behavior many of the stories were unbelievable, not worth bothering the boys with recanting of her dirty deeds.

Matteo was at Helen's house planting flowers and tending to her lawn. Helen was on the porch enjoying the cool air. When Matteo finished, he sat with Helen, she told him to tell Elena to stop making food, it's making her sick. Puzzled, Matteo asked "What do you mean, it's making you sick?" Helen explained Tonya told her that the food is too rich and high in sugar that's why Helen is not feeling well so she doesn't want any more food from Elena.

Trying in vain to explain that was not the case, that she provided only healthy meals, everything was fresh and very good for her health. There was no convincing Helen, for whatever reason she was believing everything Tonya told her. Matteo went into the house to talk to Jean and ask her about not wanting Elena's food. Jean explained it wasn't her, it was Tonya she has convinced Helen that Elena's cooking was making her sick. This while pointing out the massive donuts Tonya was kind enough to drop off for Helen.

Helen continued her newfound displeasure with Elena and moved on to her issues with Matteo. She told him that his yardwork was not good and that she didn't want him coming down to do her lawn anymore. Matteo said he's been doing it for years, why, now that his dad was gone, would she want him to stop? She told him Tonya has people that are going to come by and do it quicker and better. Again, Helen believing any of this, and where this was coming from was dumbfounding.

Elena called Helen and was stunned by her rudeness. Helen told Elena she knows her food makes her sick and doesn't want any more of that gross food and Tonya will bring her food that she needs. Elena asked Helen was there something she did, is there anything that she needs…Helen hung up on her.

Through tears Elena relayed her conversation with her mother to Matteo. He said Helen was being rude and different to him as well then told Elena about the lawn work. He knew Tonya was behind everything. She always spoke poorly about her siblings to anyone who would listen. Helen was an easy target for Tonya, she was submissive and agreeable, never confrontational, and always accepting of Tonya. It was evident that Tonya learned a masterful technique to manipulate Helen in her vulnerable state.

Matteo was determined to continue with the yardwork and Elena continued to provide meals it was the right thing to do. Driving with his tractor to his mother's home to do the yardwork he found Tonya was there with *her* crew. Tonya proudly raised her hand and displayed her middle finger while laughing then ran into the house came out with a large bag dragged a trash can to the driveway and preceded to dump the delicious untouched meals made by Elena into the trash can yelling at Matteo to "fuck off" and leave.

Jean came out and told him that Helen was paying the new crew $150 a week to do her lawn. Matteo did it for free. He went into the house to see his mother; she asked him to leave so he didn't cause any problems. The degree of manipulation on behalf of Tonya was utterly disgusting. It was evident that Tonya had been plotting this for quite some time, it was going to be a challenge to reverse the damage she has done to Helen.

Struggling to find the words to get through to his mother, she just wouldn't hear it, telling him that Tonya had everything taken care of and she trusts Tonya's decisions because she was the one who has always been there for her taking care of her and keeping her safe from the "Italians".

What has this evil, cold-hearted bitch been telling his mom? Matteo was furious he was not able to control his anger and aggressively asked "Mom, What the hell have Elena, or I ever done to you, how has anyone on dad's side of the family ever hurt you? They never have, we never have?!" He heard himself being too loud and stopped to just focus as Helen responded "See. You're always yelling." Matteo had never raised his voice to his mother, never. Helen insisted he leave her house before she called the police – which would have been Dominic, but Matteo didn't want to cause any drama he attempted to hug his mom it was a one-person hug as Helen shrugged away, he left with a heavy heart and a headful of questions. It had only been 4 months since their father had passed away and so much has changed so much of Helen has been damaged.

Matteo drove by Helen's house a short time later as Billy and his buddies were loading up Artie's 2 riding lawn mowers, a huge craftsman tool chest, table saws and other items into the back of a trailer. He called Helen to make sure everything was okay she told them they could take the stuff and not to worry about what they're doing. He was beginning to see Tonya's interest in 'caring' for their mother. Greed.

The following day Elena stopped by Helen's house and was told she needed to leave because Tonya was coming over and Helen didn't want Elena starting any trouble. Elena made every effort to talk sense into Helen, she was adamant that Tonya was the only one that she could rely on.

Jean walked Elena out the back door of the house and told her that Tonya was up to no good and was doing a lot of bad things i.e., leaving nails and tacks outside of her granddaughter's bedroom door, rifling through Jean's belongings, coming over very early and waking everyone by throwing open their bedroom doors and windows, anything to cause them discomfort. Jean also claimed Helen was missing jewelry, cash and collectible coins and the items always went missing after a visit from Tonya.

Tonya would occasionally feign kindness to Jean who at times seemed desperate for Tonya's approval and other times she behaved as though she was holding back a violent reaction. You never knew what to expect when you encountered Tonya. It was either evil, hatred, bitch, or cold-hearted snake - always manipulating.

Tonya was taking control of Helen it was so calculated she became a literal puppet master. Matteo and Elena's hands were tied they desperately tried to reach out to anyone that could speak to Helen. Tonya was deceiving Helen, she believed everything Tonya told her. She even bragged to Jean that she convinced Helen to change her will and leave Matteo and Elena each $1 so they can't contest the will. This gave Tonya great pleasure. She is just evil. All Tonya ever did was take take take.

As the months passed, Elena and Matteo continued with the phone calls that were always cut short and one-sided, sending flowers for various occasions that were never acknowledged. It was almost as if Helen now despised them and their efforts to connect with their mother angered her.

It was a cool September day when Helen received a phone call from her nephew Andrew. This was out of the blue, they haven't spoken in months ever since Martha took Helen to a casino, 'borrowing' $800 of Helen's money to gamble with, and the two got into an argument.

When Jean asked about the argument, Helen said she questioned Martha about all the times she cheated on Andrew and couldn't believe he never divorced her, she even mentioned how Martha had an affair with Andrew's brother, and may have said something about the dog, she couldn't remember everything. Okay, it was obvious why Martha was angry, everyone knew she slept around, but no one ever dared say anything. Everyone was sure that Tonya prodded Helen to say those things so she could better isolate Helen.

Andrew hasn't spoken to Helen months, so why now? Tonya told Helen that Andrew was going to take her to her doctor's appointment because he also wanted to buy her lunch. Jean insisted that was something she has always done, and that Helen wasn't comfortable going with Andrew. Tonya told her to mind her own business that she was taking care of Helen's needs and no one else knew what their mother needed.

At this point Jean just couldn't hold back, enough of all the bullshit Tonya was bad and Jean knew it. "I'm *not* going to mind my business when it comes to Mom, you're having idiot Andrew take her to the doctor appointment when that is something I have always done this isn't right. Oh and while we're on the subject about what's best for mom, where are her bank statements? She says she doesn't get them!"

Tonya insisted the doctor is a specialist that Andrew is familiar with so that's why he must take her and then claimed Helen does in fact get her bank statements, she just doesn't remember because she has dementia. Tonya told her that everything is taken care of that since no one else seems to care what happens to their mother, everything falls on her and it's a lot of work. Jean, as dumb as she was, knew a scam. The next day Jean drove Helen to the bank, she asked about the bank statements.

The teller said that Tonya provided them with a notarized power of attorney signed by Helen and took control of her bank accounts, she had the statements sent to her because Helen was no longer capable of taking care of her own finances. The teller provided Helen with a few months of canceled checks.

While going over the canceled checks Jean added up nearly **$43,000** Tonya had written to herself. Tonya paid several of her mortgage payments, a fence around Tonya's home, groceries, car payments, **liposuction,** etc.

Jean called Matteo and told him what was going on and that their mother had no idea Tonya was spending all this money. The puzzle pieces are starting to fit. Matteo called an attorney and asked what options were available. The attorney said he could go get a power of attorney and have his mom sign that one to void Tonya's power of attorney then added if Helen did in fact have the onset of dementia, she wouldn't be able to sign over power of attorney. Helen still wasn't speaking to Matteo and Elena, so that wasn't a viable option. Matteo wasn't worried about the money; he was worried about his mom.

It was time for Helen's doctor appointment Andrew picked up Helen who was almost pleased to be going to the doctor so that she could spend some time with Andrew. She did like Andrew and didn't mind his wife, she just forgot not to say anything about Martha being a whore. At the appointment Andrew was in the exam room with Helen, he handed the doctor a piece of paper as they spoke quietly. Helen couldn't hear the conversation, the doctor turned and asked Helen one or two questions and they left.

Helen said "that was an odd visit" Andrew didn't respond. In the past their conversations were spirited and fun, she thought maybe he was still holding a bit of a grudge because of something she said to Martha. Her memory was failing every now and again and at this point she couldn't remember exactly what she said, but she remembered it made Martha angry. Andrew stopped at a fast-food restaurant on the way back to Helen's home bought her a burger and dropped her off to eat alone. Helen was disappointed in the lack of conversation and felt disconnected to Andrew.

A few weeks later Andrew called and said he and Martha wanted Helen to come over for dinner. This was surprising since their last encounter seemed forced and unwanted. Helen still was uneasy with Martha and knew she didn't want to be around her, but she liked Andrew, so she begrudgingly agreed. She told Jean it didn't feel right, she felt Andrew was up to something, but didn't know what it was. Jean said he probably just wanted to get back in with the family after the argument with Martha, maybe they're just trying to be nice now or felt bad about how he treated her when he took her to the doctor. Helen insisted something was "up".

Jean did notice that her mother was a bit forgetful and chalked up her being uncomfortable around Martha because of the time Helen talked about all the affairs she had. To ask Helen why there was an uncomfortableness around Martha, she couldn't remember the reason. It was just a 'feeling'. Funny the things a person does retain, she remembered that Martha was a whore but didn't remember calling her out for it.

The Friday of Labor Day weekend, Jean and her granddaughter planned to spend the night at her daughter's house after a cookout. Knowing she was going to be drinking she didn't want to drive home. Jean told Tonya of her plans and was assured that she would be there to care for Helen upon her return from dinner with her nephew, Andrew. This was a first. Jean said she could ask Matteo's boys to come down, Tonya became angered by the suggestion. How dare anyone in Matteo or Elena's family be anywhere near Helen.

It's Friday and Tonya had not yet arrived. Jean called her and was told to leave she's on her way. Helen just then remembered she had to go to her nephew's for dinner. Jean laid out Helen's clothes and told her she would be back the next day. Tonya was on her way over. Tonya never showed up. Andrew stopped by to pick up Helen at 3:00 in the afternoon.

Andrew's house was a 25 minute drive from Helen's home. A very quiet 25 minute drive. The sad vision of this woman who didn't even want to go to the dinner being ignored made to feel as if she were a bother. Helen greeted Martha and struggled to make nice knowing that Martha was still angry about something.

They had pizza and pop for dinner. Not like they went through an ounce of trouble, inviting her over then ordering a pizza. Jerks.

It was maybe an hour or so when Andrew finally said, "Let's go!" There was a coldness to his voice that worried Helen. Martha didn't even say goodbye, she just went upstairs as if she were glad the evening was finally over. Helen managed to get to the car and put her walker in the backseat with no assistance from Andrew who appeared bothered and pleased at the same time. She remembered she liked Andrew and that he was her nephew but at this moment she more feared him than anything.

The drive home was quiet of course. Andrew was taking an unfamiliar route Helen said, "This isn't the way home" Andrew scathingly replied "You're going where the doctor says you need to go!" As they pulled into an assisted living facility Helen cried desperately. Her cries fell on deaf ears. Andrew didn't care as he unceremoniously brought her inside directing her to her new living space. Tonya was there to greet her with an exaggerated "Welcome Home!" Loathsomely glaring at Helen admiring her pain and confusion.

While at the "dinner" Tonya and her crew went to Helen's home and removed all her belongings along with some of Jean's belongings. Tonya kept for herself Helen's washer, dryer, curio cabinet filled with collectibles and the remaining jewelry that Tonya neglected to steal during her many visits when she collected her "paycheck" for fake cleaning of the home.

A distraught Helen could barely get her thoughts together, she wanted to be home. Her home. The home where she and Artie raised four children, this was wrong, everything she knew was at that home. Tonya insisted this is the best place for her whether she liked it or not. A nurse came in and gave Helen some medication, perhaps to calm her down. Helen took the medication without even thinking about it, she was going through the motions, lost in her disbelief.

Tonya told her to quit overreacting and pointed out all the trouble she went through to get Helen's belongings to the assisted living home in such a short time. There was Helen's couch, bedroom set, clothes, and even a selection of photos of Tonya, Billy, and one of Jean. She threw away any memories of Matteo, Elena, and their families.

Through her tear-soaked face all she could ask is "why?" Tonya said "Have fun" as she left Helen sitting on the couch still crying.

Helen spent the night in shock attempting to make sense the circumstances and why she was there. A nurse was kind enough to sit with her for nearly an hour to assure she would be well taken care of and talk about the assisted living home saying how she will feel much better in the morning. Thank goodness for the nurse and her concern for this poor old woman being dumped there so cold-heartedly.

The nurse wondered why the daughter treated her mother so badly, wishing she could stay longer to help Helen get acclimated to her new home, but had many other patients to care for. As she left, she promised she would stop by often throughout the evening to check on her.

The next day Jean came home to a note posted on the garage *door "Took mom to assisted living. Move out by the end of the month I'm selling the house!"*

It would be 3 days before anyone learned where Tonya and Andrew had placed Helen. The assisted living was in the next town over near where Tonya lived. Jean rushed over to see her mother, who was in her room with Tonya. Tonya was surprised that Jean found out where Helen was, yet unaffected, she knew she held all the cards. Jean cried as Tonya mockingly laughed at her with an evil glare in her eyes.

Jean told Helen that Tonya and Andrew were planning on selling her house. In utter disbelief Helen angrily looked at Tonya and said, "You will NOT be selling my home!" Tonya laughed and said "Oh we will, we need to pay for this place" Helen was at a loss, she couldn't understand why this was happening. She was happy at home, Jean and her granddaughter took great care of her, why were Tonya and Andrew doing this? Tonya had to leave to pick up Billy from the bar, she told Jean to leave or she will be thrown out.

Now that Tonya left, Jean told Helen even though she was estranged from Matteo and Elena they were getting an attorney and were going to get Helen back home. Helen was so relieved and told Jean "Please tell them I love them both so much and thank them for me". Helen's head was swirling. She knew she loved all of her children, she knew there was some reason she wasn't speaking to Elena, and Matteo, but couldn't remember what caused her to drift from them.

Jean asked why Helen would sign power of attorney to someone like Tonya. Helen said just after Artie died Tonya showed up with three friends. Well, Helen thought they were friends. Helen said Tonya said she just wanted to make sure that Helen was taken care of and told Helen to sign papers so she would be able to help Helen because she would forget things and this way no one could put her out of her home, Tonya promised she would always stay in her home, that was important to Helen, it's important to any elderly person.

The familiarity of her home that she shared with Artie for so long was comforting. She'd walk into a room and remember something about Artie, look at the kitchen and would picture him working on the windows, the memories made her smile only to be ambushed and kidnapped, yanked from her home by Tonya and Andrew was such a blatant betrayal.

Turns out those three friends that stopped by for a visit with Tonya were the 2 witnesses and a notary she needed to legalize her control. Tonya was planning this long before Artie passed away. There were just too many T's crossed and I's dotted and Tonya wasn't that bright. She had help from someone. Light bulb – this is where Andrew comes into the picture. He has mastered stealing from the elderly, i.e., his own parents, so Tonya knew he would be a good source to utilize to assist her in stealing from her mom.

Tonya had power of attorney over Helen's money and somehow Andrew got power of attorney over her health. The two scumbags were in cahoots and they knew exactly what to do. Tonya relied on Andrew to take care of the paperwork that was too confusing for her, reading and comprehension is not her strong suit.

They didn't see Jean as a threat, they felt she was an idiot and wouldn't be able to stop them from doing whatever they wanted. She lived in the home with Helen and couldn't stop them from their plan so Jean was allowed to have limited visits with Helen but had to call and arrange her visits with Tonya beforehand.

Tonya's friend, yes, she had *one,* worked at the assisted living home. Kayla prevented Matteo and Elena and their families from seeing Helen saying they were "not on the list" and were not permitted to be in the building. After a few weeks Jean was also booted out and no longer permitted to see or speak to Helen. Jean believed it was because she had mentioned Billy's kid to Helen again.

Jean didn't intentionally say things to piss off Tonya, which was so very easy to do, her mentioning Billy's son was in line with whatever conversation they were having and it just kind of slipped. Tonya's fury over someone having a child with her man was frightening. Whenever she was angry it was evident Billy would step back, avoid eye contact, and keep quiet he knew how to behave as not to get in too much trouble.

The list of eligible people that could visit with Helen was limited to Tonya, Billy, Andrew, and his tramp wife. It was heartbreaking how they sequestered Helen from her family with the help of the Assisted Living home. Tonya is absolutely a cold-hearted, greedy bitch. She has been proving that her entire life. Andrew's behavior has solidified the stories about him stealing the money from his brothers' inheritance. Greedy bastard, and Tonya obviously shared the same DNA.

The assisted living home was being paid very generously from Helen's funds so there was a strong monetary reason for them to abide by the demands of Tonya and Andrew. Elena, Matteo, and Jean called or stopped by every day and were always told they were not permitted to see or speak to Helen. The local police wouldn't get involved, saying it was a civil matter and the assisted living home is a private business.

The attorney made a lot of promises and bragged about other cases just like this one that he got favorable results from, assuring Matteo and Elena they didn't have to worry. He'd need a $5,000 deposit to get started. Matteo quickly wrote a check and said "get it done".

Dominic called the police department in the town of the assisted living home. Legally he knew they couldn't force the home to let his wife and brother-in-law see their mom, and he didn't want anyone to do anything that would compromise their job, but he needed to find out if there was any way they could help. Unfortunately, they confirmed what he had suspected, it was a civil matter and the assisted living home is privately owned. Since no crime has been committed their hands were tied. Dominic made calls to everyone he knew, and legally Tonya and Andrew covered their bases.

A week went by, another week went by. Matteo reached out to the attorney asking why the delay? The attorney said Matteo should go for guardianship and needed to provide the attorney with all of Helen's medical records. Just about impossible. Matteo had no power – Andrew controlled the medical, Tonya controlled the money. They are brilliantly evil.

After about a month of calling, a nurse answered because the receptionist took a quick break. Perfect timing. She said she didn't know how to transfer a call and asked Elena for her phone number. She said she was going to go to Helen's room and call from there so Elena would have the number. She did!

When Helen heard Elena's voice, she asked why she hasn't been calling or coming to see her. She didn't believe Elena when she said they weren't permitted. "Bullshit" Helen exclaimed. She was angry and hung up on Elena. Ladybug recognized Elena was in pain and snuggled up on her lap to offer the comfort only a dog could.

Elena called Matteo and Jean to give them the phone number to call. She explained the reaction when she had called and hoped they would get better results. Helen was more kind to Matteo but still didn't believe that he couldn't call or see her. Helen said he has no idea how horrible Elena is, saying Tonya told her *everything*. How Elena took her riding lawnmowers, tool chests, jewelry, and whatever wasn't nailed down. When Matteo tried to explain what really happened, it was in vain, Helen was brainwashed over the last few months by Tonya and Andrew.

Telling her elderly mother her family, her children, want nothing to do with her, saying they did horrible things, so Tonya could 'have it all' was something she perfected. Her cold-heart and evil ways lay the foundation for her troubled plan. She had Helen and her bank account right where she wanted.

Matteo continued to call Helen daily but then there were phone issues. It rang incessantly, Elena called the front desk and asked why her mother's phone wasn't working, they claimed the phone repair person was supposed to come out and fix it. They lied. Her number was changed.

It took quite a while to get the new phone number. Persistence pays off. After a few weeks Matteo was once again able to speak with Helen. Helen had nothing good to say about Elena, Matteo was not even allowed to mention her name. Tonya really did a job on his mother's memory. Disgusting. Matteo, Jean, and Elena all knew this was all due to Tonya and Andrew abusing Helen, her alleged dementia and their constant lies. There was nothing they could do to get through to Helen.

Matteo made it a habit of calling the attorney regularly asking about any progress that was made and what he and Elena could do. Elena paid another $5,000.00 hoping the money will get the attorney to work faster - no progress, still 'waiting for papers'.

Matteo called his mother several times a day in an attempt to get her to understand what was really going on. Problem is she had been so brainwashed by Tonya and douchebag Andrew it was an uphill battle.

Matteo still couldn't mention anything about Elena and fought to hold his tongue. Explaining to Elena his sorrow but he couldn't talk about her if he still wanted to be able to contact their mother. Elena understood that Helen was not in her right mind and that Tonya and Andrew were responsible for everything that was going on, but it didn't hurt any less. Matteo only wanted to connect with his mother and to make sure she was okay, eventually she was genuinely pleased to hear his voice.

After a few months of Tonya leaving threatening letters/notes on the door Jean received notice in the mail that she was being taken to court to be evicted. Of course this is another phone call to Matteo. She told Matteo the court date and asked if he would show up and support her in case Tonya tried something crazy – which was likely.

At the court hearing Tonya produced a notarized "Transfer of Deed" this deed was made just weeks after Artie's passing. Bitch. She just wanted everything. She was not only helping herself to Helen's jewelry, cash but now her home too. Only Tonya cared about the money, house, and belongings. They all would have gladly given her whatever she wanted if they could see their mother.

Matteo called his mother with a headful of questions knowing he had to tread lightly. After chatting about bingo, lunch, and her new friends, Matteo, choosing his words carefully, asked Helen why she signed her home over to Tonya. She said to him "That's crazy! I have four children, why would I leave *her* my house?!" Helen's burst of clarity surprised Matteo. Helen continued recalling the only papers she signed were the papers so Tonya could take care of her medical appointments and medications. Helen added Tonya brought over three friends to meet her that day.

It wasn't worth upsetting Helen to explain that those three people were two witnesses and a notary and that she had signed a Transfer of Deed and Power of Attorney. Nothing for her health, just her money.

Matteo was furious, Elena told him "it's just money. It's okay. As long as mom is healthy who cares if bitch has all her money?" Dominic was even angrier than Matteo saying "Let me find any reason, any fucking reason to lock that bitch up!" You knew when Dominic was beyond upset, that's when he cussed he was always a gentleman with masterful self-control and in his line of work that is a rarity. He said, "having that sick cow behind bars would be a dream." That dream would remain a dream. For now.

Having her mother hidden away at the Assisted Living brought Tonya happiness. It was a way of Tonya controlling everything. She had all the monetary parts of her plan covered and that wasn't enough. She wanted to cause them heartache by taking their mother away, worse yet, making their mother believe she hates all her children but for Tonya – the only one who visits her. Oddly enough with Helen's deteriorating mental capacity somehow, she never told Tonya about Matteo's phone calls. Maybe she forgot he called, or she knew that the calls would end if Tonya found out.

Tonya has been miserable since childhood which was her own doing. All the classes her mother tried to enroll her and Jean into, all the times Elena wanted to befriend her, when Matteo and Elena cooked and baked for her wedding, she never appreciated anything. She had an unwarranted sense of entitlement. Now that her plan has worked, is this going to fulfill her? Will she have a sense of purpose?

A moving truck arrived and Jean's belongings were neatly packed. No one knew why her granddaughter lived with her, she would only say their mother was in another State and the little girl didn't want to move with her. It was better not to ask.

Conrad, Jean's whatever he was, told her she could come back and live with him. She loved Conrad and was happy that she could be back with him again. Her reasons for not being with him would change with the day, he cheated, he lied, no job, he moved…Jean was an odd one, hard to read, apparently going to whomever was able to help her with her needs at that moment. When she needed a home, it was Helen, when she needed legal help, food, money, it was Matteo and Elena. Now she was back with Conrad and the granddaughter was happy to be back with her Grandpa - where things were better structured and resembled a normal family unit. Conrad was kindly indifferent to his family, giving just what they needed but no more.

Tonya's visits to Helen were less and less frequent after Helen in a subdued dreamlike state muttered to Tonya "What happened to Champ?" Tonya stayed away believing the more Helen saw her the more questions she would ask, something from this old woman's mind was coming to the forefront and questioning things that happened years ago could cause problems for Tonya. Not that anyone would believe this old lady with dementia, but she didn't want the past mentioned to anyone.

Elena and the other family members were still not able to see or speak to Helen. It was a painful heartbreak they would never understand. Nor would Helen. Matteo continued his calls, not mentioning Elena or anyone that would upset Helen's frail mind.

Tonya was now able to access Helen's home. She had already cleaned out all the belongings and treasures but was hoping for one final score. The sale of the home there was a small issue with selling the house. As it stood now, Tonya had the paperwork that showed she would get the home if Helen should pass away "Transfer of Deed", if she sold the house before Helen died, the money would go to the Assisted Living home.

Tonya also had Power of Attorney over all of Helen's money and created a "Joint" bank account. She was hoping to put the money from the sale of the house into that account and claim it as her own. She needed to do a bit more research to see if this is something she could get away with.

Her coworkers at the bank started talking about the things she was doing since Artie passed away. They all felt something wasn't on the up-and-up, she wasn't well liked at the bank but she did her job, so she was left alone. No one was willing to answer any personal financial questions, she bragged too much about having control over her mother's money which made the coworkers feel uncomfortable.

Easter was just a week away, Elena and Matteo sent Helen the most stunning flower arrangement to the Assisted Living home. When Matteo called Helen, she excitedly talked about the amazing flower arrangement Tonya and Billy had given her.

That fucking bitch took the flowers and claimed they were from her. Should have expected she would. This is the dumb kind of bullshit she has always done. Just a nasty bitch. Matteo only responded how thoughtful that was of her then to Helen's surprise he described the bouquet in detail. "How did you know?" Helen curiously asked. "I sent you one just like it, I hope you get mine too." Helen thanked Matteo and told him she was excited to receive two beautiful bouquets. She only received the one.

Just weeks following a lovely Easter celebration, the families prepared to celebrate Moms. Of course, the restaurant was packed with happy Moms, delicious food, and laughter. Elena's kids loved to celebrate Mother's Day and Dominic always spoiled her more than he should. Anita and Matteo had a beautiful celebration with their sons then came to the restaurant to enjoy appetizers and a glass of wine while Ladybug played with the kids on the patio. Despite not being able to speak to her own mother, it was a lovely day for Elena filled with family.

It was the Monday following Mother's Day, Matteo just pulled into his driveway from work when received the call. It was Andrew "You're gonna save a lot of money on flowers, your mom died yesterday." What the fuck?! Matteo was shocked, then angry and before he could say a word Andrew hung up. Fucking coward.

Gathering his thoughts Matteo went into the house and told Anita, they weren't sure if it were true so they had to call the Assisted Living their response was "She's no longer a resident here" and wouldn't elaborate on whether she had passed.

Matteo called Dominic who was able to make a few calls and learned that Helen, in fact, had passed away. Dominic was angry at how the news was delivered to Matteo, the flagrant disrespect for decency, the mockery by Andrew was repulsive.

Dominic's friend Charlie was a lead detective the one who filled Dominic in on the details. Charlie was close to Elena too and enjoyed several meals at Cibo with Anna, they met at the soft opening of the restaurant and were still dating occasionally so he was well aware of Tonya and her deceitfulness.

Charlie was determined to find out every little detail of what happened and although Helen's passing was initially thought to be an "accidental" drowning while taking a bath, he told Dominic he's going to quietly investigate this, so no stone is left unturned.

Charlie went to the assisted living home and told the administrator that no one was permitted into Helen's room until he was done with a thorough inspection. The administrator told him "old people die all the time", Charlie told her "Good to know. Stay out of the room until I am done with my investigation, or you will be arrested." This scared her enough that she assured compliance.

Not sure what to look for he was methodic taking photos of everything in the apartment including medicine, the food in the refrigerator, the bathroom, clothes hamper, he was systematic and thorough. He enlisted the help of a few coworkers to ensure he didn't miss anything – including fingerprints.

Charlie told Dominic that since Andrew had Power of Attorney over her health, he and Tonya attempted to rush for a burial, but an autopsy was being done and the coroner knows to take special care of his mother-in-law.

Dominic let Matteo know what Charlie was going to do and they agreed *not* to share the information with Elena or Anita, they believed it would be another level of pain that was unnecessary.

Tonya with all of Helen's money was to oversee the funeral arrangements but of course she was too lazy and heartless. She had Billy call and tell Matteo he would have to take care of it, and she would reimburse him for the funeral costs from their mother's account.

Matteo and Elena were pleased to honor their mother's memory by providing her a lovely ceremony and burial next to Artie. The one demand from Tonya is that there be no food provided by Cibo and the guests meet in the church's basement for sandwiches.

Elena brought in food from Cibo disguised as food from Tonya's deli of choice. It was a quiet gathering heavy with sadness for all the time Matteo, Elena and their families didn't spend with Helen because of Tonya and Andrew.

Dominic and a few of his law enforcement friends kept a close eye on Andrew, Billy, and Tonya to make them uncomfortable. Matteo made it a point to walk up to Andrew while Dominic and his friends circled Andrew so Matteo could land one solid punch.

Matteo grabbed him by the throat angrily whispering, "You sick piece of shit, you're not worth killing but damn I hope you die a miserable death". Dominic quietly stepped back and got in between the two and warned Andrew to stay away from their families.

Andrew hurriedly grabbed his whore wife and left with tears coming down his face as he sniffled in a handkerchief while blood dripped from his face, the coward couldn't get out of the basement fast enough.

Tonya and Billy took advantage of the distraction Andrew provided and packed up several bags of food leaving without a word to anyone.

Tonya never paid for the funeral, Matteo and Elena didn't expect that she would. Greedy bitch.

A few weeks after the burial, Charlie brought Dominic and Matteo along with him to talk with the coroner. The coroner told them that normally if a person fell asleep in the tub, they would wake up as they started to breathe in the water – their body would kick into survival mode. However, Helen's blood results showed an elevated level of diphenhydramine, a drug commonly found in sleep aids.

The amount of sleep aid in her system prevented Helen from waking. The water eventually filled her lungs, causing her to drown and because she was under water for an extended period, without prompt resuscitation, irreversible neuronal cell injury along with the development of hypoxic-ischemic encephalopathy resulted in cardiorespiratory arrest. Laymen's terms, she took too much, or was given too much, sleep aid, and fell asleep and drowned.

Charlie asked Matteo if there was a reason his mom needed medicine to sleep. Matteo said as far as he knew, she never took anything, she was always able to sleep well. The nurse that was assigned to Helen confirmed she never took a sleep aid, and when she saw Helen the evening before her passing, she was in good spirits and ready for bed. Not a bath.

Could she have been given the sleep aid without her knowledge? Charlie asked the coroner. The coroner stated there are many sleep aids that can be melted or crushed and hidden in a meal or a drink.

Charlie combed over the myriad of photos and bagged evidence finding nothing that would cause Helen to fall asleep. Nothing in the trash, nothing in the medicine cabinet, refrigerator, there was nothing there that would explain how she could have taken something to make her fall asleep.

Dominic had to share the news with Elena and Anita. Understandably they were beside themselves in disbelief and anger it was horrible enough to lose Helen, but to have possibly been intentional is incomprehensible.

Dominic assured them Charlie and all his law enforcement connections were going to get to the bottom of this and find out what really happened. Dominic may have involved Charlie out of spite for the way his wife had been treated or a sense that something didn't add up, maybe both. He was so grateful that he made that call and so grateful for his friends and their expertise in getting answers.

Charlie went to the assisted living home and greeted a very nervous Kayla who was on the verge of tears. Charlie asked why she was so nervous? Told her she wasn't under arrest, wasn't being detained, there was no reason to be nervous. She started crying and told him she doesn't want to talk to him.

Charlie told Kayla he would get to her later, but for now wanted to speak to Ms. Velky, the administrator and to page her immediately. Kayla called Ms. Velky with a shake in her voice told her to come to the front desk, the police were there. Charlie knew Kayla was a weak link in Tonya's arsenal and would be easy to break and planned to delve further into her connection to Tonya later.

Time for Charlie present his search warrant to the administrator, Ms. Velky. Charlie enjoyed showing her the search warrant signed by a Judge allowing him full access to whatever he needed from the property. She was aware what a search warrant was and quickly complied as not to alert the other residents that anything was amiss.

Kayla immediately called Tonya to tell her the police were asking questions. This enraged Tonya who quickly called Andrew to discuss their alibis and bafflement on anyone being interrogated over the death of Helen.

Charlie obtained the video footage of every person who entered Helen's room the day before her death, the day of and the day after her death. The only people to have entered Helen's room were a nurse for a brief visit at 8:12 pm the night before for her regular wellness check. Helen could be seen in the doorway in her bathrobe and slippers – confirming as the nurse had stated, Helen was readied for bed, not a bath.

Tonya was there at 8:50 pm the night before Helen's death staying until 9:03 pm a thirteen-minute visit, locking the door behind her. Tonya returned with Andrew at 7:37 am the morning of her death staying until 7:53 am. Helen was found by the nurse in the tub at 8:40 am.

Charlie and his coworkers watched the video several times each finding something new with every view. It was evident that Helen was alive after the visit from the nurse at 8:12 pm as Helen is seen closing the door behind the nurse. Tonya let herself out of the apartment at 9:03 pm carrying an empty green plastic grocery bag that she balled up in her fist. The next morning when Tonya and Andrew left at 7:53 am there was visible "wetness" on Andrew's khaki pants and a spattering of wet spots followed Tonya's footsteps.

Charlie returned to the assisted living home, he wanted to trace every step Tonya and Andrew took. He needed to find out what was in the grocery bag and to see if she discarded the bag somewhere on the property. His coworkers went to the nearby drug stores and supermarkets where they looked through records to see if Tonya or Andrew had made any purchases of melatonin, diazepam, or medicines that would cause someone to become sleepy.

It took several officers and several stores later before they were successful in their hunt. Tonya had purchased Melatonin gummies and an antihistamine that contained Diphenhydramine two days before Helen's death. She used her rewards card and paid for the products with her bank card.

The officers were able to get the security footage showing her walking the store, they almost laughed when they noticed she stole a few candy bars. There she was picking up the melatonin and antihistamine, headed to the self-checkout, paid with her bank card then put the products in a green plastic grocery bag.

Charlie had Dominic come to the precinct so he could show him all the evidence and the case they have built up against Tonya and Andrew. Tonya bought the medicine, gave it to Helen the night before, or put it in her breakfast, Andrew came the next morning to help Tonya put a sleeping Helen into the tub, drown her then left, leaving the nurse to find her later that day.

Charlie and his coworkers went through the painstaking steps of going frame by frame of the video showing Tonya arriving with the green bag to the nursing home just 7 minutes after purchasing the drugs. The outline of the antihistamine could be easily depicted when the video was enhanced.

Tonya can be seen leaving with the green plastic bag balled up in her hand as she tosses it into a trash receptacle. They needed that trash! Charlie went to the assisted living home and spoke with Ms. Velky. It's been weeks but is it possible the trash is still there? It was. The assisted living home only pays for trash to be removed once per month. Gross.

Thankfully Charlie's coworkers were more than happy to sift through the mounds of diapers, food, and nasty to find what they needed – the green plastic bag! Still containing Tonya's receipt!

It was shocking to learn that Dominic's hunch paid off, he didn't want to be right, and it was going to be hell to have to explain to Matteo and Elena what had happened. Charlie and his officers were readying themselves to arrest Tonya and Andrew for murder. Dominic was going to head to the restaurant, he asked Matteo to meet him there in about 2 hours so he can talk with him and Elena together.

The kids were in school, Elena was doing her usual morning restaurant chores the paperwork and payroll was complete.

Dominic called and told her he was stopping by soon with Matteo, he needed to share what Charlie had found out.

Her heart sank, she knew that Charlie was looking into what really happened to her mom, she could feel her heart sinking. She headed into the dining area to start her cleaning and prepare for Dominic and Matteo's arrival, she wanted to stay busy so she wouldn't over-think.

Pulling the framed photos from the walls for a thorough cleaning, Elena admired every crevice of every frame and the memories they held – her mom, her dad, her grandparents, love.

As she reached for the next photo her head was smashed with a heavy force causing her to fall to the ground. Dazed and in utter confusion, she was forced on to her back then immediately straddled, her understanding of the events that were transpiring were clouded she knew she was hurt and something was wrong but couldn't make out what was happening.

It took a moment for Elena to recognize it was Tonya that had straddled her swallowing Elena's delicate frame with her enormous girth. Elena's left arm was pinned under her, she was unable to move. Tonya's fingers were fat like marshmallows yet the grip on Elena's neck was strong. As she was squeezing the life out of Elena as she boasted how she enjoyed killing Champ. "That stupid dog, it fought for a bit, but I choked the life out of that mutt in 5 minutes flat. That made you cry, and I laughed so hard.

You and Matteo crying over a fucking dog. Now you have something in common with that Mutt, I'm killing you the same way! I've always hated you; you always thought you were so perfect, you're a fucking bitch! Do you hear me?!"

Elena was fading, it was as if a movie of her life was playing in her mind. She was playing with Champ, she loved him so much. She was drifting in and out of consciousness opening her eyes to see the ring of sweaty clumps of dirt between the rolls in Tonya's neck. She prayed this is not the last thing she sees in her life. The movie of her life began again she saw David, the tree fort, the orchard…

Tonya continued "David, poor little David, he should have known it wasn't you on the phone inviting him to the cliffs you two assholes spent so much time together. Stupid boy might still be alive if he would have just done what I told him. He thought he was too good for me, tried to leave I grabbed him, and he pushed me away, I punched his stupid face he tried to knock me out of his way and scratched me, pushed me into the trees, when I saw my knee bleeding, I knew that was the end of him. My push was much better, he went right off the cliffs I laughed at him as he was laying there bleeding. You were so sad boo-hoo your stupid little friend was dead."

Tonya continued for what seemed hours "You've always got everything you've ever wanted; you spoiled fucking bitch! Daddy loved you best, you're so pretty, fuck you! Now you're dead! Now I have everything, I have the money, I have the house, I have everything!"

Elena passed out then came to, she was dying. Her life continued in her head, all her memories, all her loved ones, every person she cared for and everything she would miss. These would be her final breaths she was coming to peace with the fact that her life was over she wouldn't see her children again as a tear rolled from her soft eyes following the curve of her cheek she prayed for her family.

A loud shrill scream pierced Elena's final thought, suddenly she was able to gasp a magnified breath of air. The screams were falling from above, the echoing sounds of confusion filled the restaurant the source of the screams were perplexing they weren't coming from Elena, she didn't feel dead but was sure Tonya had killed her, yet she could now move her arms, the weight was off her.

She opened her eyes to see Ladybug ferociously attacking Tonya. Ladybug, her sweet dog who wasn't allowed into the restaurant area broke the rules and came in from the patio to save Elena's life.

Tonya was grabbing tablecloths, candles, chairs anything she could to hurt Ladybug. Gathering her thoughts, processing what was happening Elena looked up and saw Artie's photo. The strength that radiated through Elena was a gift from Artie, it had to be the sudden burst of strength was unexplainable. Springing to her feet as if she wasn't just nearly killed, Elena grabbed Tonya by the hair and smashed her head onto the wooden table.

Tonya's fat head bounced off the table as a trickle of blood ran down her fat face she lost her balance fell to the ground and Elena stomped on her stomach. Tonya rolled a few times to get away from Elena's assault she stood up quicker than expected for such a large woman. She flung around now trying to fend off two attackers. The table didn't do enough damage, but Elena was just getting started. Tonya had the look of a demon radiating from her eyes her evil face grappling to resemble something humanlike.

Her leg had the most pleasing bite marks which tore through her ill-fitting jeans exposing a gruesome bite and hanging flesh. Elena made a fist and struck Tonya square in the jaw just like Dominic taught her to punch causing the fat pig to fall to the floor once again. Ladybug pouncing on the opportunity to get back into the fight leapt on her fat legs and chomped down one last nasty bite. Elena ordered Ladybug to lay down and stop, she reluctantly obeyed while anxiously continuing to keep Tonya from Elena. Elena grabbed a chair and held it over her head, this was going to be a painful blow and she took pleasure in being the one to deliver it.

The chair was now heavy and wouldn't move…Dominic was holding the chair back from Elena. She turned to her husband and fell into his arms as Ladybug ran over to the two of them to make sure Elena was okay. Matteo came in and quickly assessed what was happening he pulled Tonya up by her mop of hair, gave her one solid slap across her fat ugly face and said "Be glad that's all I do to you, you fat fucking bitch!"

Dominic sat on the floor cradling his wife as she cried and hugged Ladybug. Matteo called for an ambulance so Elena could be checked out and told them to send a paddy wagon for fat ass. The police officers arrived just as the ambulance pulled up, Elena was placed on the gurney and gently placed her in the ambulance even though she insisted she was fine.

Dominic didn't have to say a word to anyone they were his friends, and everything was going to be handled. Matteo placed Ladybug in his truck as the officers put Tonya in handcuffs and in the second ambulance. She had some serious bite wounds that Ladybug proudly and bravely caused and some obvious injuries to her face and head. The EMTs didn't exercise tenderness when loading her up. They did the bare minimum. Which was more than she deserved.

When they loaded her up in the ambulance she was screaming "That damn dog needs to be put down, it bit me! I'm suing!" Ignorant of all the hell she was in and how all her efforts to steal her mom's money was fruitless. She wouldn't be getting a cent, she will, however, be enjoying 'three hots and a cot' for the rest of her life behind bars.

When the police arrived at Andrew's house to arrest him for the murder of Helen, they banged on the door and heard a gunshot. They quickly drew their guns and called for backup and an ambulance. Moments later the front door to the home quickly opened and Andrew rushed out with his hands up. He had planned to kill himself, instead the coward killed his wife then surrendered to the police.

He was a weak man attempting to share his alibi saying his wife pulled the gun on him and he took it and killed her by accident, and it was Tonya that killed Helen, not him. The officers quickly cuffed him as he cried they were on too tightly. They told him to shut up then read him his rights twice after he claimed not to understand the first time. They wanted to make sure there was no question this piece of garbage was punished as severely as legally possible.

The coroner arrived and loaded up what was left of Martha. Good riddance.

Tonya was stitched and bandaged then swiftly taken to her temporary jail cell until after her trial when she would be moved to a less comfortable cell.

Elena spent the night in the hospital because Dominic wanted to make sure every inch of her was perfect like she was before Tonya attacked her plus he knew she would benefit from being cared for a bit longer by the nursing staff.

Elena came home the next day greeted by a houseful of family, she quickly covered her children in kisses, hugged her aunts, cousins, brother and sister-in-law then scooped up her hero Ladybug and cried. If not for Ladybug, the outcome would have been very different.

Dominic bought too many bouquets of tulips, the kids made a cake, Aunts made their eggplant and the cousins all supplied delicious foods. Elena sat on the couch with her children snuggled as close as they could while Ladybug spotting a small opening squeezed in offering sloppy kisses to her devoted family to which they gleefully accepted.

The kids were so happy to see their mom they didn't want to leave her side but were soon coaxed to play outside with their cousins and Ladybug. Dominic was quick to claim the spot next to his wife and wrapped her in his strong, protective arms. It was the most comforting feeling to be in the arms of her husband. Aunt Maria brought them both over a plate of food while Aunt Giana poured the wine.

The adults were talking briefly about what had happened, they told Elena that Dominic had shared the restaurant's security tapes with them, so they knew everything that Tonya had done before Helen. Elena had forgotten about the security cameras and was so thankful that Dominic insisted on getting the absolute best security system, it picked up everything that Tonya had confessed to and everything that happened.

It was easy to see why Ladybug was getting extra special attention from everyone they saw her save Elena's life. Again, so thankful that Dominic and his K-9 friends gave Ladybug some training. Although, Ladybug loved her family so much it may have been instinctual to stop whatever was hurting someone she loved. Whatever the case, Ladybug was a hero.

With the security tape confession about killing David, the evidence from the Assisted Living home and Kayla's written statement testifying that Tonya told her she had planned to "off" Helen - when she did, she would buy Kayla a car, the purchasing of the sleep aids, there was more than enough evidence to find her guilty. She tried in desperation to blame Andrew who in turn tried to blame her, which after killing his wife it was a hard sell.

Tonya's court-appointed attorney had an earful from Tonya about the vicious attack from Ladybug and how she was beaten and abused by Dominic, Elena, and Matteo. She was quickly reminded about the restaurant's security tapes and the attorney was quick to accept a plea deal, 30 years in prison without the possibility of parole.

Tonya glanced around and spotted Billy. She was so happy he came to show his love for her, she wasn't the brightest bulb in the lamp. He was there with his son and his son's mother. His last and probably only "Fuck You!" to the bitch that was so controlling. By the grotesque look on her angered face, if she could, he would be her next victim.

Jean and Conrad were there for the spectacle of it all and were shameless enough to get Tonya's attention just to flip her off and laugh at her. This was a murderer, not just a murderer the person who killed your mother.

Elena, Matteo, and their families knew Tonya had accepted the plea deal so they decided not to go to the hearing. It was over. She's going to prison. They'll be safe now and can move on with their lives.

There would be no trial for Andrew. He was raped in his jail cell then hanged himself. After hearing about this, Matteo said to Dominic you know my dad "knew a guy". Dominic said, "I don't wanna know!" then offered a salute to Artie as he and Matteo clinked their wine glasses together and gulped a mouthful of Artie's favorite wine.

The next day everyone went to visit the gravesite of Helen and Artie. The kids brought fresh flowers and took turns reading aloud from a book to their grandparents. Ladybug lay on Artie's